The Patriot Wore Petticoats

Based on the true story of "Daring Dicey" Langston

By Marnie L. Pehrson

First Edition 2004

Published by CES BUSINESS CONSULTANTS
Copyright 2004 Marnie L. Pehrson
Cover design by Tammie Ingram
Cameo cover art and "Dicey Meets Thomas"
original artwork by Janis Wilkey

A historical fiction novel based on the life of Laodicea
"Daring Dicey" Langston, a Revolutionary War heroine.
Dicey was born May 14, 1766 and died May 23, 1837
http://www.DiceyLangston.com

Printed in the United States of America

ISBN: 0-9729750-4-7

To Luanna

*my treasured friend who believes in me
when I lose faith in myself,
who makes me laugh when I feel like crying,
and who loves Dicey almost as much as I do.
Thanks for everything, Lu!*

In Loving Memory

*of my great aunt Thadda Estelle Springfield Moody
July 22, 1915 - February 15, 2004*

Chapter 1

"So we meet at five tomorrow morning at the North ford of the Enoree?" asked the short, stout man, his pug nose crinkling as the sun streamed through the trees and into his eyes.

"Yes and bring the Kilmer brothers with you. I'll see that the rest of the Scouts are there. We're going to eradicate these rebels amongst us if it's the last thing I do. We'll attack Little Eden at dawn," replied Bill Cunningham, with a glint in his eye. The tall, attractive leader of the Bloody Scouts would normally be the type of man that made a girl's heart skip a beat, but his exuding ruthlessness repulsed any woman with a shred of discernment.

Laodicea Langston clung with her back to the opposite side of a large oak no more than four feet from the two men. "Dicey," as her friends and family called her, withheld a gasp and raised her hands to her mouth. *James and his men are at Little Eden!* she thought to herself. Panic sent her heart pounding within her chest. She'd promised her father no more spying – no more carrying messages she overheard to the Patriots. But it was hard for Dicey. In this war, anyone could be a Patriot or a Loyalist. Because women were rarely given notice – and especially young women like 15-year-old Dicey, she often stumbled upon interesting conversations. Well, *stumbling* would be a bit understated. The first conversation Dicey overheard was purely by accident; but soon she found that if she kept her eyes and ears open and maneuvered herself discreetly at parties and community events, she often heard important information that would help the Patriot cause.

While Dicey clung to the side of the tree waiting for the men to clear the area, her mind shot back to the conversation with her father only a month before.

"Dicey, I understand what you're trying to do. James and Solomon are part of the Patriot forces and it's understandable that you're worried about them. I'm concerned about them too. But your brothers are fighting for our liberty and we have to trust that the good Lord will take care of them. You can't go eavesdropping all over town and carrying messages to your brothers."

"But Papa, surely you have said yourself that God helps those who help themselves. Dare we stand idly by and do nothing, expecting our liberties to be protected while we know that our fighting men are in danger?"

A sympathetic expression flickered across Solomon Langston's green eyes. After all, he had taught his sons and daughters well. He had conscientiously indoctrinated his children that "Where the Spirit of the Lord is there is liberty" and "faith without works is dead." Could he now stand before his daughter instructing her to relinquish the beliefs their family espoused? A look of resolve crossed the tall man's brow as he smoothed his hair back with his right hand and his left stroked his neatly trimmed gray beard.

He took in a deep breath and in a kind but resolute lowered voice explained, "Now Dicey, you're absolutely right, but in this case my hands are tied."

"Whatever do you mean your hands are tied?"

"While out in the orchard this morning, two men with scarf-masked faces grabbed me from behind, held a knife to my throat and informed me that the Tories were aware of your spying and carrying messages to the Patriot forces. They demanded that I either take control of my 'feisty meddlesome daughter' or I would be held personally responsible. They even threatened to inform the Bloody Scouts of your activities so they could take care of the situation. And you know what that means, Dicey. When the Bloody Scouts take care of a situation, you're as good as dead and you'll be blessed by the Almighty if your family doesn't join you!"

Dicey threw her hands to her mouth in astonishment and gasped, "The Bloody Scouts! Papa, I had no idea! I'm so sorry for putting you and the family in danger!"

Solomon continued, "I know you meant no harm, Dicey. I know you were just trying to protect your brothers and help the cause, but this has to stop for the safety of us all."

Dicey's mind darted to the tales she'd heard about the barbaric deeds of Bill Cunningham and his Bloody Scouts. She could hear the deep, animated voice of her father's friend, Judge J. B. O'Neal., as he sat in her family's home spinning yarns about Bill Cunningham and the Bloody Scouts. The family sat musing together one evening about why these men

were so bloodthirsty. "How can they be so barbaric?" her
mother had pondered aloud.

The judge settled into his seat, took a deep breath and
began his explanation, "Rumor has it that in 1775,
Cunningham enlisted as a private soldier in the service of the
State of South Carolina, in a company commanded by
Captain John Caldwell in Colonel Thomson's Regiment of
Rangers. He served with credit; so much so, that Captain
Caldwell planned to promote him over the head of his own
brother, William Caldwell, who belonged to the same
company. Some trivial offense prevented Cunningham's
promotion, and sent him before a court-martial. They
sentenced him to be whipped. He suffered the degrading
punishment and with his blood boiling with revenge, he
deserted the flag of his country and fled to Florida. While
there, William Ritchie kicked Cunningham's aged father out
of his home. Somehow Cunningham heard about his father's
plight and swore that he would seek the blood of his father's
oppressor. He shouldered his rifle, and mostly on foot,
traversed the country between St. Augustine and Laurens
District; and in Ritchie's own house, in the presence of his
family Cunningham shot the man dead."

Dicey's and Henry's eyes widened but remained riveted
on Judge O'Neal's every word as he continued, "Upon the
first taste of blood, Cunningham developed a lust for it like a
lion's unquenchable thirst for prey. Since then, he has been
the most merciless of the Tory bloodhounds, scouring the
country, hunting to the death all those who fight for freedom
against British tyranny. He started with those with whom he
had served and were responsible in one way or another for

his court-martial. For Cunningham, revenge is a sweet elixir that nourishes his wicked soul."

Dicey jerked from her memories back to reality by the sound of breaking twigs and rustling bushes. Startling and quickly turning her head to the right, she saw a fawn rummaging for berries. She exhaled a sigh of relief, reached down into the pocket of her apron and pulled out her grandfather Richard Bennett's pocket watch. Grandfather Bennett died when Dicey was only three but she remembered sitting on his knee as a little child playing with Grandpa's pocket watch. She had been so fascinated with it that her mother decided that Dicey should have it – to help her remember those few memories that remained of her grandfather. Dicey's mother, Sarah Bennett Langston, presented it to her on her twelfth birthday. Since that time, Dicey kept it with her always.

I'm nearly an hour late! It's already half past two! Now if I can just make some excuse to leave Liz's party early. I simply must determine a way to warn James. But for now, her best friend was waiting for her.

~*~

Elizabeth Williamson, catching a rare moment to herself, stood near the fireplace in the spacious parlor of the Williamson plantation house and surveyed the guests at the party held in her honor, "Where is that Dicey?" she muttered to herself. "She's always running off when I need her." Elizabeth, Dicey's childhood friend, was a tall, beautiful young woman with long, naturally curly blonde hair that fell in ringlets to her waist. Her pale blue eyes and long eyelashes strikingly accented her porcelain features. This was an important day for Elizabeth and she needed her friend beside her. Elizabeth's father, Richard Williamson, was a likeable fellow but an avid Loyalist who was determined to find a suitable Loyalist husband for his lovely daughter. "None of that rebel rabble for my Elizabeth" he insisted.

Elizabeth's sixteenth birthday party was the talk of the town. Every eligible bachelor and every unmarried young woman in the surrounding area of Laurens District, South Carolina attended. Her father conscientiously saw to it that Patriot males were not in attendance, but that didn't limit the choices much. Laurens District was primarily Loyalist territory. What few Patriot men there were in the district were off fighting for either the Continentals or the militia. Dicey's own father had fought with them until his leg was severely wounded – leaving him to walk the remainder of his life with a cane.

Mr. Williamson wasn't so worried about the young women who were invited. While he felt Dicey to be entirely too outspoken in her Patriot views, he saw her as most men perceived women of the day – keepers of the hearth and home, but having no brains for politics or the real problems that men folk discussed. No, Dicey was no threat to Richard Williamson's mind.

Elizabeth turned abruptly as she felt a tap on her shoulder. "Dicey! Where on earth have you been? You were supposed to be here an hour ago!"

"Uh… well, I was unavoidably detained."

"Off gallivanting through the forest, I see," Elizabeth deduced, noting a twig in Dicey's chestnut hair, and her mud-caked shoes from the recent torrential rains. Elizabeth picked the twig out of Dicey's French braids and smoothed a stray strand of her friend's hair back where it belonged. "I swear, Dicey Langston! You have the opportunity to meet every eligible bachelor in Laurens District and you're off playing with rabbits in the woods."

"Liz, I assumed it wasteful to arrive on time since every young man's eyes would be fixed only upon you. I thought I'd give you an hour to select your victim so that I might choose from your leftovers." Dicey winked at her friend.

"You know I haven't a bit of judgment where men are concerned, Dicey. I'm not selecting a man until you give your approval" laughed Elizabeth.

At that moment Dicey pointed her eyes toward Elizabeth's right, directing her attention toward a young man who strode up beside them. Elizabeth turned to face the gray-blue eyes of 18-year-old Samuel Holton. He took Elizabeth's hand, bowed his sandy-blonde head and kissed her fingers gently.

"Miss Elizabeth, I'm honored to be invited to your party this fine spring afternoon. I'm Samuel Holton and this is my – uh – friend Mr. Matthew Love."

"Lovely to make your acquaintance," Elizabeth responded, pretending that she didn't recognize him. She had secretly hoped that Samuel Holton would accept her father's invitation to attend her party and could barely contain the elation she felt as he actually stood before her kissing her hand. Elizabeth turned to Dicey, "This is my friend Miss Laodicea Langston."

11

"Nice to meet you, Miss Langston," Samuel Holton who was stocky fellow just Elizabeth's height, greeted Dicey as he took her delicately small hand and then released it.

"Langston?" queried Matthew with one raised eyebrow. He continued to glare down into Dicey's striking chocolate brown eyes that were accentuated by long, thick lashes. He quickly forced himself to sweep away an expression of irritation and took her hand, kissed it and with forced politeness quipped, "Nice to meet you, Miss Langston."

At his touch a cold shiver ran up Dicey's spine. That look in his eye – what was it she wondered? While he appeared an ordinary looking fellow of medium build, the expression in his eyes exuded a mixture of what could only be described as contempt and hunger. This man was no good. She felt it instantly.

"I'm sorry, but I must leave early this afternoon. May I call on you for a stroll tomorrow morning, Miss Williamson? Your father has already given his consent," asked Samuel with a hopeful twinkle in his eye.

Elizabeth's eyes darted to Dicey who gave a subtle nod. "Why of course, Mr. Holton, that would be lovely."

"Until we meet again, Miss Langston," stared Matthew Love as he tipped his head toward Dicey and then Elizabeth.

As the two young men walked out of earshot, Dicey whispered to Elizabeth, "That man makes me physically ill."

"Who? Not Mr. Holton, I hope?"

"No, that Matthew Love. There's something evil about him. I can feel it."

"Really? He does seem a bit intense, but… What do you think of Mr. Holton?" Elizabeth held her breath hoping he met with Dicey's approval. Dicey had a rare gift for sizing up anyone. She could sense a person's true intentions and Elizabeth had come to rely on her friend's uncanny ability.

"Oh, he seems like a nice enough fellow. But he evidently is a poor judge of character or he wouldn't be associating with such rabble."

Elizabeth breathed a sigh of relief. At least Dicey had no disquieting feelings about Mr. Holton. Elizabeth felt simultaneously disappointed that he had exited her party so soon, but elated at the prospect of being the object of his sole attention the following morning.

Dicey watched her friend as suitor after suitor approached her, asked her to dance or sat talking with her. Occasionally a young man would stride up to Dicey to introduce himself and ask her to dance, but nothing to compare with the attention showered on Elizabeth. Rather than be envious, Dicey was genuinely happy for her friend because courting, socializing, and the finer things of life were important to Elizabeth. But Dicey wasn't impressed or concerned with all of that. She enjoyed nature, riding through the woods on Gabriel, hunting with her brothers, and listening to her father and brothers discuss the war and the fight for freedom. No, Dicey didn't care about the frivolous things of life. She was too contemplative for that, but she loved that Elizabeth could make her forget about the perils that threatened her family. *If everyone were as kind, loving and lighthearted as dear Liz, there would be no war, nor tyrants*, Dicey thought to herself.

As Dicey stood, gazing admiringly at her friend who could be so lighthearted and beautiful when the world

13

around her wreaked with hostility, Dicey remained completely oblivious to her own down-to-earth beauty that exuded from the confidant integrity of her soul and permeated out through her deep brown eyes. Yes, Elizabeth was beautiful, prim and proper, but there was a genuine inner beauty and grace about Dicey that would capture the heart of some young man who could look past the occasional windblown hair of Dicey Langston, the bold and reckless rider and expert shot.

Dicey could only take about an hour and a half of socializing. She approached Elizabeth, rubbing her temples with both hands, "Elizabeth, I've got a bit of a headache. I'm going to head home now."

"So soon?"

"I'm sorry, I just really need to lie down."

"Would you like to go upstairs and rest in my room?"

"No thank you, I just want to go home to my own bed. I feel like sleeping on through the night."

"I'm sorry you're feeling poorly, Dicey." Elizabeth gave her friend a quick hug, "Go home and get some rest."

"Stop by the house tomorrow afternoon and let me know how you enjoy your outing with Mr. Holton" Dicey winked at her friend.

"I will!"

~*~

On her way home, Dicey determined that she would take a short nap, sneak out after everyone had retired for the evening and ride out to warn James. As she entered the farmhouse, the sounds and smells of dinner time filled her senses – the delicious combination of fried chicken, gravy and biscuits. Sarah Bennett Langston had mastered the culinary arts and she'd been passing those skills on to Dicey. It was Dicey's responsibility to make breakfast for the family bright and early each morning. She wondered whether she could reach Little Eden and arrive home in time to cook breakfast.

As she opened her pocket watch noting the time as now half past four, she knew she'd do well to catch an hour of sleep before dinner. Her mother called from the kitchen, "Dicey, is that you? How was the party?"

"Fine mother – perfect as always. Liz would stand for nothing less. Even mother nature ceased her torrential rains to offer up a perfect day for Liz's birthday," Dicey answered with a wearied smile.

"Dicey, you look troubled. What's wrong?" her mother queried as she emerged from the kitchen wiping her hands on the white apron tied about her waist.

"Oh, nothing, Mother. I just have a bit of a headache. May I lie down for an hour or so and have you wake me for dinner?"

"Certainly, dear, you go ahead and lie down and I'll send Henry up to wake you when the food is ready," her mother comfortingly put an arm around her daughter's shoulder and directed her up the stairs toward her bedroom.

Sleep remained elusive for Dicey. Too much weighed on her mind - too much planning to be done. What would be the fastest route to Little Eden? How would she get Gabriel from the barn and ride away without anyone noticing? Or perhaps she should venture on foot? What would she do if her father or mother noticed her leaving?

Dicey breathed deeply. *I've got to relax. I have to get a little sleep or I won't make it through the night…Please Father in heaven, help me get some rest and help me arrive at Little Eden to warn James and the settlers before the Bloody Scouts do!"* she began to pray in her mind as she lay sideways on her bed with her knees tucked up to her chest.

After a short time, sleep came and went quickly and she awoke to a knock at her door. "Dicey, Mama says it's time for you to get up and come to dinner." Her twelve-year-old brother Henry stood at the door. Dicey could hear the giggles of little Celin, Bennett and Amy as they rubbed against her bedroom door.

"How many of you does mother think it takes to wake me?" she laughed.

"Oh, I thought I might need reinforcements to drag you from your bed. Celin, Bennett and Amy are prepared to tickle you while I hold you down," chuckled Henry.

"Indeed! You think you can hold me down Henry Langston?" Dicey challenged as she rose to her feet, crossed the room and opened the door. As the door swung open Celin, Bennett and Amy gathered around her legs and began tickling Dicey's waist.

"Why you're just a scrawny little thing. Doesn't look like they need me to hold you down!" observed Henry, who towered a full foot taller than his older sister.

"Come along you three, I'm hungry and I feel much better now that I've had a little rest. Let's go eat." Dicey pulled Amy up into her arms and shifted the white-haired, rosy-cheeked

16

child onto her hips while she grasped four-year-old Bennett's hand and led him downstairs for dinner. Henry took seven-year-old Celin by the hand and followed them.

~*~

After dinner, the little ones ran off to play, leaving Solomon and Sarah Langston with their two older children who were still at home – Dicey and Henry. Their older brothers, James and Solomon, were off fighting in the war, and naturally as the conversation usually did, it turned to the events of the day.

Henry Langston cleared his throat and began, "Little David Tinsley told me that his pa, Major Dunlap, and John Cummings were the only survivors of a Bloody Scout raid yesterday afternoon."

"Oh my!" exclaimed Dicey as she quickly glanced into her father's eyes which returned a somber gaze.

"It seems that they started at Commander John Caldwell's home. They shot him dead right there in his garden and charged their horses in and out of his garden in fiendish sport! Then they torched the home leaving poor Mrs. Caldwell there to cry over her husband's body!"

"When will this madness end!" exclaimed Sarah Langston, her deep brown eyes moistening with tears.

"That isn't all of it Mama. They say that William Caldwell came to Colonel Hayes in his blacksmith shop, pointed to the smoke rising from his brother's home, and warned Hayes to flee. Hayes only replied that Cunningham had too much sense to come there. William Caldwell replied, 'I will not stay

17

here to be butchered' and then he mounted his horse and fled at full speed.

Everyone's eyes strained intently upon dusty-blond-headed Henry as he continued, "As William Caldwell rode out one end of the field, he saw Cunningham's Scouts come in the other. Hayes and his men were taken totally by surprise. They were driven into the house and John Tinsley struck a full blow with his sword at Colonel Hayes as he entered the door. Shots were fired and one of Cunningham's men was killed. One of Hayes' men died in the house from a ball shot between the logs. Then the Scouts lit the house afire."

"Hayes and his men surrendered and Cunningham pulled aside Hayes and Major Daniel Williams – you know Major Williams don't you Papa? His father Colonel Williams fell at Kings Mountain."

Solomon Langston nodded his head in recognition as grave concern puckered his brow.

"Anyway, Cunningham took Major Williams and Colonel Hayes and prepared to hang them when Major Williams' younger brother Joseph ran up to Cunningham. I guess he thought he could have his brother spared since he'd known Cunningham his whole life. He pled, 'Captain Cunningham, how shall I go home and tell my mother that you have hanged brother Daniel?'"

"Cunningham instantly swore that Joseph wouldn't have that horrible duty to perform and strung him up right alongside the other two men! Can you believe that Papa? Can you believe he'd hang a boy he'd known his whole life?" Henry turned incredulously toward his father.

"They're a murderous lot, Henry. They are like the good book says, 'past feeling.' I think they don't care an ounce about this war. They just want an excuse to murder people."

"I say they're possessed by demons" interjected Sarah Langston.

"Evil, plain and simple – just evil!" Dicey gasped.

"You know what is even more appalling? The pole broke from the weight of the three men so Cunningham took his sword and literally hewed them to pieces! While wiping his sword, he saw that one of his men had – in cutting a man to pieces – broken his sword. Cunningham gaily handed him his own, commenting that his sword wouldn't break!"

The women gasped and Solomon shook his head in disgust.

"Like I said, James Tinsley, Major William Dunlap and John Cummings were the only survivors of Hayes' party. They say their lives were spared by one of Cunningham's Scouts at the peril of his own life.

"Who was it, Henry? Who let them go?" asked Dicey.

"I don't know. David Tinsley didn't say. I thought perhaps it could have been their kinsman John Tinsley, who is one of the Bloody Scouts, but he said it wasn't him. 'Twas another man he did not know."

"This is just so horrible!" exclaimed Sarah looking at Dicey, "We must do something for poor Mrs. Caldwell! Where is she staying, Henry, do you know?"

"I hear she's staying with her sister," answered Henry.

"Dicey, you and I will go there tomorrow for a visit. And we'll pay our respects to poor Mrs. Williams! Can you imagine losing two of your sons the very same day! I know it won't help much, but we'll do what we can to comfort the poor women." Sarah Langston turned to her husband, "This is entirely unsettling. I'm feeling ill just thinking about it. Let's retire early tonight, try to get our minds clear of the matter and get some sleep."

Dicey wondered to herself who in their right mind could relax and sleep after hearing such a horrific tale. But she felt relieved when her father agreed with her mother and they began preparing the children for bed. Now more than ever, she knew she must warn James so that he and his men could alert the settlers at Little Eden. Her family retiring early for the evening would give her more time to reach the settlement.

Chapter 2

After giving her family and servants ample time to fall asleep, Dicey checked her watch and noted the time as nine o'clock before reluctantly laying Grandfather's pocket watch on her night table and extinguishing the lantern. She wished that she didn't have to disobey her father, but there was just no one else she trusted to send in her place. Her brother Solomon had recently returned to his home on leave to be with his wife Elizabeth who had given birth to their first baby, Solomon Bennett Langston. But it was closer to warn James than it was to travel to Solomon's house in the opposite direction. There was no time for delays. She determined that she must make haste directly to James, and so she crept down the stairs, into the kitchen and out the back door.

Dicey pulled her shawl snugly around her shoulders and tied her scarf over her head as she entered the crisp April night air. Fortunately, the rains had not returned this evening as they had in recent nights. Dicey studied the half moon, which would be her only source of light for her secret journey. Clouds partly shrouded the gray sky and she hoped that they would let the moon continue to give its light.

21

She had decided that she couldn't afford to ride Gabriel or carry a lantern. She couldn't risk her family or the neighbors hearing hoof beats or seeing the light. It was paramount for the safety of her family that no one knew she had warned the settlement. She walked briskly, following the main road toward the Tyger River. Daring not to travel on the road itself, she paralleled at a distance that would insure she wouldn't be seen by passersby.

She knew that she must pace herself yet venture quickly for it was at least eight miles to the Elder Settlement at Little Eden. James and his men were just outside the settlement. She would find James and have his men ride to warn the settlers as she returned home before anyone discovered her absence. Dicey had traveled this route several times to take messages to James, but it had always been by the light of day. Everything seemed different at night and the sounds of coyotes howling in the distance and other animals rustling about her in the woods added to her nervousness.

Occasionally she stubbed her toe on a tree root, and stumbled forward attempting to regain her balance. She crossed marshes and creeks along her way, and her boots and the bottom of her dress were soon soaked. *What I wouldn't give for a lantern!* she thought as she crossed a small creek, hopping from one stone to the next, slipping and landing on one knee, bruising it severely.

As she continued along her journey, she tried to keep fearful thoughts at bay by counting her blessings. After all, it could be raining, but it wasn't. Her father, mother or one of the servants could have seen her slip away, but evidently they hadn't. The moon gave enough light to see her way.

Mostly, she felt grateful that she had happened upon Bill Cunningham and his accomplice in the forest on her way to Liz's party. What if she hadn't overheard that they were planning to massacre the settlers at Little Eden? All those people would be dead and one of them would most likely be her brother!

She decided that she had been blessed and that if the good Lord saw fit to lead her to this information, He would help her reach the settlement in time and unharmed to deliver it. She walked briskly and traveled in a timely manner until she reached the hill overlooking the river.

Suddenly she let out an audible moan as a feeling of panic seized her. The ordinarily deep river now swelled beyond its banks from the recent rains. She knew it would be high, but hadn't considered that it would be this deep. From the top of the hill she overlooked the river, trying to decide where would be the best place to cross. Through the dim moonlight she saw the ford and decided that she must wade through it.

That looks like it's over my head! She thought to herself. Dicey stood scarcely five feet tall so crossing a swollen river in the middle of the night was not what she had bargained for. *Oh My! Isn't there some other way?* She searched her memory for an alternate route to Little Eden that did not require crossing the Tyger, but she could think of nothing and could see no other available option. A sudden engulfing loneliness gripped her as the seriousness of the situation settled over her. Weighing her options, Dicey resolved at last, *I must do this. There is no other option. I've come this far and if I can cross this river, then James and the settlers will be spared, but if I fail, all is lost.* A thousand horror stories of the Bloody Scouts and what they did to settlers raced through her mind. This morning, she resolved, they would have no blood to spill.

Carefully, she worked her way down the hill toward the river's ford. She knew she needed heavenly help to accomplish her objective. As the hoarse rush of the waters competed for her thoughts, she dropped to her knees in the rain-soaked grass, ignoring the pain in her bruised knee as she prayed for the strength and agility to meet the challenge. As she concluded her prayer, a verse from the New Testament entered her mind, "I can do all things through Christ which strengtheneth me." *Lord, be with me and strengthen me. As Mother always says, 'With God nothing is impossible!'*

She knew she couldn't cross the river in so many layers of petticoats, so she removed her skirt, stripped off her petticoats and folded them along with her shawl into a neat roll in hopes that she could hold them above her head to keep them dry as she crossed the river. Clad in her bloomers, she stepped into the water and startled with the force of the rushing river that threatened to sweep her away. Her heart pounding, she took another step, it swirled up to her thigh already and she had barely gotten started. As she waded out farther, the freezing waters reached her chest. She held her roll of dry clothes over her head in an effort to keep them dry. Then as if Satan and his minions were determined to hedge up the way, the clouds rolled over to deny her the only source of light she had. The darkness reigned complete and she took another step, only to feel her body plummet. Her head plunged under the icy water, and she scrambled frantically to find her footing, saturating her roll of clothes as she did so.

Finally her foot caught hold of the river bottom, and she stood with the water up to her neck. Gasping for air, pitch darkness surrounded her and Dicey no longer knew which way to go. She'd somehow gotten turned around when she plunged under the water. Fearing that her next step might plunge her deeper until the water rose entirely over her head, she carefully wandered in the channel, peering and straining about her searching for a clue as to which direction to travel.

Lord, help me to find the way! James and the settlers must be warned! Surely you didn't bring me this far to drown?! Then her heart caught hold on the verse that had reassured her earlier, "I can do all things through Christ which strengtheneth me." She repeated it over and over, calming herself down enough to regain composure.

Finally she felt a quiet assurance that she must turn to the left and walk forward. She followed the prompting, carefully wading in the designated direction until she reached the riverbank. Exhausted, with her heart pounding, she collapsed on the grass. As the clouds rolled away from the moon, she could see that she had indeed landed on the correct side of the river. *Thank you, Lord! Thank you!* her heart cried out in gratitude as she looked heavenward. Dicey lay there a minute or two regaining her composure and then decided she had lost too much time in the water. Without Grandfather's pocket watch, she had no idea how long she'd wandered aimlessly in the channel, but gratitude filled her heart that she'd had the foresight to leave it at home on her night table. She had known that she would need to cross the river, and that it wouldn't be safe for the watch, but she had no idea just how unsafe it really would be.

Dicey did her best to wring the water out of her bundle of clothes, rose to her feet, and put her petticoats and skirt back onto her freezing body. They felt like lead weights hanging about her as she headed in the direction of the settlement, continuing her journey through the woods. Her teeth chattered as she wrung the water from her shawl and scarf as she trudged onward. While the items were of little use to her now, she knew she must take them with her, so she tied the shawl back around her shoulders and shoved the scarf into her pocket. Dicey reached behind her head and wrung the water from her waist-length braids.

Walking briskly for both warmth and speed, before long Dicey reached James' camp. As she entered the encampment, dozens of haggard and worn men were entering from the opposite direction. Dicey strained to make out the faces coming toward her until she recognized James. Quickly she ran to him and threw her arms about his waist.

"Dicey! What on earth are you doing here in the middle of the night? You look like a drowned kitten, little sister!" her brother exclaimed as he pulled her back to examine her face.

"I had to come, James! It's the Bloody Scouts. They're going to attack the Elder Settlement at Little Eden. I overheard Bill Cunningham and one of his men planning it for dawn."

James quickly grabbed one of his men, "John, we must warn the Elder Settlement; Dicey's overheard a plot for its attack at dawn. The Bloody Scouts are on their way. Gather the men and we'll send them out in different directions to warn the settlers."

John shook his head, "James, the men are exhausted and hungry from their excursion. They're not going to feel like getting back on their horses now and riding off again."

"Well, I'm not having the blood of those settlers on my head. I don't care how tired we are, we're going to sound the alarm."

Men started to gather around them to discern the source of the commotion. The sheer exhaustion on their faces filled Dicey's heart with pity. "Gather some wood and start a fire and fetch me some corn meal, flour and oil if you have it. I'll make something for the men to eat while they ride," she directed.

Eager to pacify their grumbling stomachs, the men dispersed in various directions and quickly they stripped a few boards from a lean-to and started a fire. In short order, Dicey cooked a hoe-cake.

"I'm sorry it's not baked completely through, but we simply don't have the time for a proper meal," she apologized as she broke the cake into pieces and gave each man a wedge to put into his shot pouch. "You can eat as you ride," she explained.

James gave her a quick embraced, "Thank you Dicey! I take it Papa doesn't know you've come?"

"No, no one knows," she assured him.

"Then leave now. You should have plenty of time to make it home, but you don't want to take any chances."

"I will."

James mounted his horse, started forward, then turned back toward her, "And be careful crossing that river!"

"I will, James. I will!"

The men rode at full speed, traveling from house to house warning the settlers of the impending attack. Families gathered their children and evacuated their homes in the dead of night, taking only a few personal items that they would need for the next few hours. As the men sounded their warning, Dicey began the eight-mile trek back home. Yawning, stumbling and shivering she reached the Tyger River.

By this time, the clouds had dissipated. The moon and even a few stars were shining brightly. With trepidation, she removed her shawl, skirt and petticoats, rolled them up, and stepped back into the river and waded slowly across. This time she kept her bundle of clothing in the air as she crossed. When she reached the other side, she dressed and continued toward home. By the time she reached the farmhouse, darkness still pervaded the land and everyone slept. She crept back in through the kitchen door, up the stairs and into her bedroom.

Dicey immediately approached her nightstand, lit the lantern and checked her watch – half past four. The servants would be up milking the cows soon. She'd made it in the nick of time. Dicey quickly stripped off her wet clothes and put on dry ones. The warmth of the dry clothes on her body filled her with a secure comforting sensation. *It's over! It's so wonderful to be home!* She felt like tossing herself on her bed and sleeping the entire day away, but she knew she couldn't do that.

Her father would be rising soon and would want his breakfast before going outside to work. While she had a little

bit of time, she knew if she let herself relax, she'd never wake
up.

Dicey yawned, stretching her arms high above her head,
and moved to her washbasin. She lifted her small looking
glass and studied herself in the mirror. *"What a mess!"*
Dipping her washcloth into the water, she wrung it out and
removed the mud that caked to her small nose and high
cheekbones. After she had thoroughly cleansed her face and
neck, she loosened her braids and sat down on her bed and
began brushing her wavy chestnut hair. She swooped her
long, thick tresses into a swirl on the top of her head and
returned to her dresser. *I need a good bath,* she thought to
herself as she studied the face in the mirror once more. *But
this will have to do.*

Dicey stepped to her night table, picked up her pocket
watch and placed it back home inside the pocket of her clean
apron. With her lantern in one hand, she opened the door to
her bedroom, and then proceeded down the stairs and into
the kitchen.

She decided to make a big breakfast for her father since
she had plenty of time. Lighting the wood burning stove, she
then added a couple of logs from a nearby woodpile, and
then scooted a step stool across the room with her foot until it
lay directly below a row of cabinets. Stepping up on the stool,
she still strained to reach the upper row of cabinets that were
well over her head. She pulled down a bowl, and the various
ingredients she needed to make biscuits.

After mixing the biscuits, rolling, cutting and placing
them into the oven, she ventured out in the yard to hunt for
fresh eggs. She carried a lantern out with her and set it on a

flat stone to illuminate her search for eggs. The laying hens roamed the yard and laid their eggs wherever they found a comfortable nesting place. One of the hen's favorite spots was just outside the kitchen door, behind a board that leaned against the side of the house. Dicey squatted down to peek behind the board, and sure enough, there were two freshly lain eggs. She continued to check the hen's favorite spots and gathered the eggs into a basket until she had over a dozen eggs. *One or two more should be enough,* she calculated.

She stooped down, set the basket of eggs on the ground, and began searching for another egg in a clump of hay, when suddenly she felt a hand cover her mouth and an arm encircle her waist from behind. She struggled for freedom, but the arms were too strong and the man behind her, who stood at least six feet tall, caught her off balance and pulled her into the air with her feet off the ground. *Did someone follow me home? Are the Bloody Scouts onto me?* she frantically interrogated herself.

Struggling to scream, she halted when a familiar deep voice assured her, "Dicey, calm down, it's me – James."

Instinctively she still struggled for freedom. "Shhhh, Dicey, it's me – your brother James."

Once she ceased fighting, he loosened his grip enough to allow her to spin around. As she did so, she discovered that indeed her older brother, James, stood before her. A handsome young man of twenty-three with chestnut hair the same color as his sister's, James had his father's green eyes while Dicey had her mother's brown - only Dicey's eyes were a deeper chocolate brown that almost looked black at times.

Dicey angrily gazed up into his face as she pounded her fists on his massive chest. "What in the devil are you doing? Trying to scare me to death?!" she agitatedly whispered.

"I'm sorry. I didn't want everyone to know that I'm here. I can't stay but a few minutes. I came to ask you a favor."

"A favor? I shouldn't do anything for you. I risk my life crossing that abominable river to save your skin and you repay me by frightening the life out of me!" Dicey retorted in a loud whisper.

"I know. I'm sorry, Dicey. Your bravery does require that I thank you for what you did. You saved a lot of lives this morning. I just wanted to make sure you arrived home safely."

"As you can see, my dear brother, I'm safe and sound," irritation still seethed through her voice. "So what's this favor?"

"I need to leave an extra rifle here. There's another regiment that's running low on munitions and I have this extra rifle, and I need a place for them to pick it up."

"So who shall I give it to?" she questioned as her fists and the muscles in her face began to relax.

"I'm not sure exactly who will come for it yet, so I can't give you a name. You'll know the man you need to give it to when he gives you the password."

"That seems easy enough. What *is* the password?"

"It's musket men."

"Well isn't that original!" her chocolate eyes laughed at her brother, allowing the dimple on each cheek to escape. "So when should I expect this mysterious musket man?"

"Could be two to three weeks. They're fighting over in Lancaster District and will be working their way in our direction to join with some troops at Woods Fort," James answered. "I need to leave now. I want to make a quick stop to see Beth," he continued as he handed Dicey the rifle.

"I hope you're kinder to your poor wife than you've been to your sister this morning! Don't be sneakin' up on her like you did me!"

James' eyes brightened as he threw both arms about his sister, pulled her close and kissed her brow, "Thank you Dicey for everything. Be careful," then he turned and walked away.

Dicey glanced around to make sure there were no surprise visitors awaiting her, stooped and grasped an egg from the furrow of hay. Placing it gently in her basket, she rose and entered the kitchen door, carrying her basket in one hand and the rifle in the other. She set them down and then stepped outside to quickly retrieve the lantern and brought it back into the house. From the kitchen window she gazed toward the explosions of red, orange and pink as the sun dawned a new day.

~*~

Wild beating horse hooves raced through the Elder Settlement. Sixteen men led by Bill Cunningham scattered in pairs to make their assault on the unsuspecting citizenry. Bill Cunningham kicked his boot into the front door of the most prominent cabin of the settlement, knocking it down and leaving it hanging precariously from its upper hinge. Each pair of men worked a similar attack on seven other cabins throughout the vicinity.

One man carried a rifle, while his companion bore a torch as each pair scoured their chosen home, vandalizing, taking whatever they found valuable and shoving it into their sacks.

"There's no one here," Matthew Love called to Cunningham. Similar observations were made by their comrades. William Parker called out the front door of a small two-room cabin, "There's no one here either!"

Jonathan Kilmer yelled to his brother William, "The ashes are still smoldering in the fireplace. Someone's warned them to leave!"

Pairs of men poured out of the cabins and met in the center of the main street. "Who in the devil leaked that we were attacking this morning?" exclaimed Bill Cunningham with a venomous scowl.

Each man shook his head and denied that he had any part in the matter. "Well, someone leaked it! An entire settlement doesn't evacuate for no reason!" he bellowed. "Torch them all – every last cabin!" he exclaimed. "Take what you will and torch them!"

"But what if they aren't all rebels?" a tall sandy-haired man queried.

Cursing a string of expletives, Cunningham commanded, "To the devil with them! Burn it all. There's not a one of them fit to live, much less keep their property."

Fiendish howls wrenched the air as the incendiaries ransacked the cabins, mounted their horses, and tossed torches atop each roof. Within minutes Little Eden stood as

silent and empty as that ancient Eden after Adam and Eve
were driven out of the garden.

~*~

Dicey carried the rifle to her bedroom and glanced around
for a place to hide it, finally placing it under her mattress. As
she exited her room, she met her father in the hallway.

"Good morning, Papa," greeted Dicey with a smile.

"Morning, Dicey. Something sure smells wonderful!
You've been up early, have you not?"

"Yes, Sir, very early," she answered.

As she and her father entered the kitchen, Sarah Langston
stood at the stove stirring the gravy and glanced back over
her shoulder. "Dicey's prepared a feast for us this morning,
Papa," Sarah Langston's deep brown eyes wrinkled into a
smile and an expression of gratitude and admiration spread
across her face.

"Hmmm... scrambled eggs, biscuits, gravy, sausage, and
fried apples!" Solomon smiled as he rubbed his stomach with
his hand.

The tromping of footsteps sounded overhead as Henry,
Celin, Bennett, and Amy descended the stairs and scurried to
the table.

As everyone settled around the table, the night's
escapades began to catch up with Dicey. Exhaustion gripped
her body and mind and she sat down in front of her breakfast
– not so much because she felt hungry as she was afraid if
she didn't sit, she'd collapse.

Dicey sat in a daze as her family engaged in daily conversation.

"It's a beautiful morning. I thought we'd go for a ride to visit Mrs. Caldwell and Mrs. Williams this morning, Dicey," commented Sarah as she looked out the kitchen window.

Dicey continued to stare toward the window, not acknowledging that anyone had spoken to her.

"Dicey, did you hear me?" her mother questioned.

Dicey's blank gaze persisted. Finally Henry waved his hand in front of her face, "Anyone alive in there?" he laughed.

"Dicey, are you well, dear?" questioned Sarah

"Oh, yes, I'm sorry. What were you saying, Papa?" Dicey shook her head and turned to look into her father's face.

"I didn't say anything, my dear. Your mother wants to know if you would like to go with her to visit Mrs. Caldwell and Mrs. Williams this morning," answered her father with a puzzled expression.

"Oh, I uh –"

"You don't look well, Dicey," noted her mother.

"I'm sorry Mama, Papa, I – "

"You didn't sleep well last night, did you Dicey? You look like you didn't catch a wink!" Nothing got past Sarah Langston where her children were concerned.

Sarah rose from her chair, approached Dicey and placed the back of her hand on her daughter's brow, then leaned forward to press her cheek to it. "You feel a bit warm, Dicey. Off to bed with you!"

"I'll go after I clear the dishes."

"No, Henry and Celin can do that. Off to bed with you now. I'll have your father take me to see Mrs. Caldwell and Mrs. Williams."

"It would be safer if I take you anyway, Sarah." Solomon surmised.

As Dicey rose from her seat, left the room and climbed the stairs, Sarah turned to Solomon, "I'm worried about her. After Elizabeth's party yesterday, she came home and took a nap. That's not like her and now this morning she seems so distracted and exhausted."

"She's probably just coming down with a cold," Solomon reasoned. "Dicey's a strong girl. She'll be fine."

"I suppose, but still…"

Upstairs in her bedroom, Dicey collapsed on her bed and fell asleep within moments.

Chapter 3

Dicey awoke to a knock at her door. "Dicey, are you awake?" she could hear Henry's voice from the other side of the door.

"Just a moment, Henry," she answered as she rolled over and grabbed her pocket watch from the night table. *It's nearly three! I've slept the whole day!*

"Liz is here to see you, Dicey. Do you feel up to it?"

"Yes, please send her in, Henry." Dicey sat up in her bed, straightened the comforter in front of her and tucked a stray strand of hair back into its place.

Elizabeth tapped on the door and slowly opened it. Peeking her head in the door, she asked, "Dicey, may I come in?"

"Yes, Liz, please do."

"Henry said you weren't feeling well?"

"I'm much better now. I just needed some rest," she yawned. "So what brings you here this afternoon?"

"You asked me to stop by and tell you about my walk with Mr. Holton this morning," Liz smiled.

"Oh, that's right! Yes, please do tell me all about it! You're smiling, so I suppose that means you had an enjoyable visit?"

"Yes, very enjoyable!" answered Liz with a far away look in her eye.

"My dear, Liz, you look absolutely smitten," teased Dicey.

Liz blushed and feigned conservatism, "It's too early for all of that, Dicey."

"Don't pretend to be level headed with me now, Liz. I know you better than that! Tell me all about it."

Smiling, Liz relaxed her facade and excitedly began to relate the events of the morning, "He arrived at our house shortly after breakfast. Of course, Father was extremely happy to let him in. Mr. Holton is from a well-respected Loyalist family, you know. And that's always paramount for Father."

Dicey rolled her eyes, "Of course..."

Liz continued, paying no mind to Dicey's cynicism. "Lilly chaperoned as we took a walk in the garden. He is just so handsome, Dicey! And so remarkably entertaining! Did you know that his family raises prize winning horses? He's been to New York and Boston and told me all about his adventures there. We walked and talked for at least two hours! He's visiting me again Saturday afternoon."

"That's just wonderful, Liz! I'm so happy for you!" Dicey exuded honestly. While the fact that Samuel Holton came from a prominent Loyalist family would be repugnant to Dicey, she knew that Liz did not fret about political matters. Liz would be happier and life would be easier for her if she chose a man who met with her father's approval.

"Mrs. Elizabeth Holton. The name suits you," Dicey winked.

"My word, Dicey! It was just a morning's walk," Liz pretended that the thought of marrying the handsome Samuel Holton had never crossed her mind.

"Oh that's right... I forgot." Dicey teased.

"So, tell me Dicey, what has you in your sick bed?" Liz held the back of her hand to Dicey's brow. "You don't feel warm."

"You're as bad as mother, Liz. I'm fine. I just didn't sleep last night and it all caught up with me today."

"Didn't sleep? Why not?"

"Oh, just a lot on my mind with the war and everything. I worry about my brothers, you know."

"It must be ever so frightful to have two brothers in the war. It's times like these I'm happy to only have sisters." Liz rose from the side of Dicey's bed, "I will leave you now to rest. I just had to stop by and tell you about the morning."

"I'm so glad you did, Liz. It sounds delightful! I'll see you at church on Sunday and we'll walk home together afterward so you can tell me all about your next meeting with your Mr. Holton."

"Yes, that will be perfect!" agreed Liz as she gave her friend a quick hug and walked toward the door. "I hope you feel yourself again soon."

"I'm feeling better already. You always brighten my day, Liz."

The two young women smiled at each other and Liz waved slightly as she left the room.

Dicey wondered whether she would ever find a young man who suited her and held the same strong patriotic values that she did. That young man would be harder to find

in Laurens District than Samuel Holton had been for
Elizabeth. She shrugged the thought out of her mind and rose
from her bed, straightened her hair and dress and started
downstairs.

~*~

Billowy white feather pillows floated in the azure sky and
bright rays of sunlight punctured them, streaming through to
heat the afternoon. Two weeks had passed since Dicey had
warned the Elder Settlement without anyone realizing that it
was she who had made the midnight run to save them. Dicey
straightened the parlor, cleaning the furniture with a feather
duster when she heard the pounding of horse hooves outside
the house. She set the feather duster on an end table and
bolted to the window. Holding the curtains together and
peaking out, she counted four men who dismounted and
tromped up the front porch steps to stand before the front
door of the Langston plantation house. A tall handsome
young man who appeared to be Dicey's age led the group.
His torn, rolled-up shirtsleeves which exposed his well-
formed biceps accentuated his muscular build. The four men
had evidently recently seen battle as their worn and dusty
clothing hung on them and their bodies were bruised,
scraped and cut.

The leader approached the front door and knocked firmly.
Dicey put her hand to the door, "Who is it?"

"This is Lieutenant Thomas Springfield. My men and I are
from the twenty-first regiment of the South Carolina militia.

We've come to retrieve a rifle that your brother James left for us."

Remembering the rifle she had hidden under her mattress, she motioned to Henry at the top of the stairs to keep Celin, Bennett and Amy upstairs with him. Their mother and father had gone into town for supplies and left Dicey in charge of the children.

Dicey unlatched and opened the door a crack and looked up into the young man's kind eyes. He tipped his hat from his blonde head and his deep blue eyes locked into Dicey's chocolate ones. He seemed so familiar to her. For a moment, there remained nothing in the world but those beautiful blue eyes staring into hers. She noted the dimple in his strong chin and a cut in his left cheek. She wondered what battle had caused such a gash and resisted the urge to reach up and soothe away the pain that it must be causing him.

A shorter, stout young man standing to Thomas' right cleared his throat, "The rifle, Miss. Do you have it?"

Dicey tore her eyes away and looked to the speaker. "Yes, come in." She opened the door wider and the four men stepped inside the home. "Have a seat there in the parlor. I'll get the rifle."

Dicey sprang up the stairs and toward her bedroom. Opening the door, she paced to her bed and pulled the rifle from beneath the mattress. Breaking herself from the spell of the young man awaiting her downstairs, she realized that she had neglected to ask for the password. How did she know that these men were not Tories in disguise, determined to steal the gun?

Original Artwork by Janis Wilkey

She held the rifle in a ready position and carefully descended the stairs. Two of the men had seated themselves in the parlor while Thomas Springfield stood facing the staircase awaiting her return. A fourth man studied a portrait of Solomon Langston that hung above the mantel.

"You four don't look like militia men. I will need the password as proof that you are who you say you are," she ventured as she stepped down to face Thomas Springfield, looking determinedly up into his piercing eyes.

"It's too late to make conditions, Miss Langston. The gun is already in our possession and its holder too!" teased Thomas Springfield with a twinkle in his eye and the dimple in his chin deepening.

"Do you think so?" she exclaimed defiantly as she cocked the rifle and held the muzzle to his heart, "If the gun is in your possession, take charge of her!" Dicey's pulse raced and she wondered whether the possible danger of the moment caused her heart to pound so wildly or the thrill she felt from Thomas Springfield's gaze.

Thomas studied Dicey's expression and the determination it held quickly erased the smile from his face. He began to wonder if he'd misread her. He felt certain that she was as enamored with him as he was with her, but now he second-guessed himself. Could this beautiful little lady really be serious?

Deciding she threatened in earnest, Thomas raised his arms slightly to attempt to quell her vexation with a position of surrender. His deep voice soothed, "Now there, Miss Langston, I will give you the password. Just put down the rifle."

Dicey didn't flinch as she continued to hold the muzzle to his heart, "The password, Sir."

"The password is musket men, Miss Langston," Thomas acquiesced.

Dicey disarmed the rifle, lowered it from his chest and handed it to him.

"You certainly are worthy of being James Langston's sister!" bellowed the heavy-set fellow who had been relaxing on an ottoman by the window. The other two men nodded in agreement and approached the pair. Thomas extended his hand to her, grasped it gently yet firmly and kissed her fingertips. "Yes, you are a brave young woman. It's an honor to make your acquaintance."

"I'm glad she's on our side!" laughed one of his friends, "She really put you in your place, Springfield!"

Again, she found herself lost in those deep blue eyes and fought to tear herself away from his gaze as his three companions started heading for the door.

"We'll be leaving you now, Miss. Thank you for the rifle and for a royal display of bravery," boomed the heavy set man as he slapped Thomas on the back and pushed him toward the door.

As the four men started to exit, Dicey held the door open and watched them mount their horses and gallop away. Just before going through the gate, Thomas Springfield turned back over his shoulder, tipped his hat and smiled at Dicey who stood gazing out the front door. She returned a dimpled smile and nodded. As the men rode away, over the hill, and out of sight, Dicey continued to stare in their direction, secretly wishing the rugged young man with the wavy blonde hair and penetrating blue eyes would return. Finally, she shut the door, bolted it, and turned to lean her back against the door. She released a sigh and wondered if she would ever meet him again.

With her back still to the door, she heard a knock. Thinking that the liberty men had returned, she spun around, unlatched and opened the door with a smile spread across her dimpled cheeks. The smile quickly fled, as horror replaced the anticipation of seeing Lieutenant Springfield again. Tory Captain Gray with his riflemen loomed before her.

She struggled to shut the door, but the men were too strong, barged in, and flung the door so forcefully that it nearly burst from its hinges.

"Well, well, Miss Langston, so nice of you to invite us in!" the sinister man mocked.

"Get out of our house! You have no right to be here," she demanded as she pushed at his chest with all her might, but she may as well have been pushing against a hundred-year-old oak for all the progress she made against the looming invader.

"Better watch yourself little lady, or my men will take more precious valuables from this house than just your property."

The man and his two companions burst forward and began grabbing anything of value from the house and thrusting it into their sacks. Captain Gray and his riflemen were what were commonly referred to as "cowboys" – basically thieves who used the war as an excuse to loot their neighbor's property all in the name of loyalty to king and country.

Dicey hoped that Henry and the little ones would remain hidden upstairs until the men left and prayed silently that nothing more than their property would be harmed. As she caught sight of a large burly man climbing the stairs, she held her breath and the blood rushed through her veins like a raft flailing recklessly down a rushing swollen river.

Upstairs the man began knocking things about as Henry lay under his bed, the little ones crowded around him. Henry

45

put his forefinger to his lips instructing the children to be quiet. He bit his lip and held his breath, his pulse racing as he peered toward the door and saw the man's boots stomping into the room. Henry's eyes widened in panic as he realized that Bennett's foot was sticking out from under the bed. Quickly Henry reached over and tugged the child's pant leg to bring it beneath the bed. Bennett inhaled deeply and Henry quickly put his hand over the little boy's mouth to keep him from making any noise.

The boots approached the bed and stopped directly in front of Bennett's face. The little child's eyes clenched shut and it felt like hours before the boots finally scuffled away. Satisfied that there was nothing of value in Henry's room, the man turned and proceeded to the next room.

Downstairs, a filthy looking man with a long scraggly black beard, picked up a large pewter basin from an oak library table in the parlor, "What about this, Capt'n? Reckon it's worth takin'?"

"Perhaps — not sure whether it's worth lugging back with us though."

"It might bring a price in the marketplace," suggested the man, turning the basin over examining it from all sides.

"Let's take it," settled Captain Gray, "We can run it into bullets to kill the rebels," he added with a sickening smirk and a defiant glare in Dicey's direction.

"Pewter bullets, sir," answered Dicey, "will not kill a Patriot."

"And why is that?" inquired Captain Gray with a menacing smirk.

"It is said, Sir, that a witch can be shot only with a silver bullet; and I am sure the Patriots are more under the protection of Providence than any witch would be under the care of her devilish master."

"Indeed, well we shall see, won't we, Miss Langston?" He snatched up the pewter basin and thrust it into his bag.

"I see little else of value here. Let's be on our way." He reached his hand forward, squeezed Dicey's chin between his thumb and fingers, and pressed his face close to hers. The nauseating stench of liquor on his breath caused Dicey's stomach to churn as he warned, "Tell your father, Miss Langston, that if I did not have such respect for him, he would have found one additional pretty little precious possession spoiled this day. Next time neither he nor you shall be so fortunate."

Releasing his grip on her chin and thrusting her head to the side, he shoved her until she lost her balance and fell to the floor. With a disgusted glance in her direction, he raised his hand into the air and motioned to his men to follow him. They stomped toward the door, out into the yard, mounted their horses and rode away.

As soon as they were out of sight, Henry ran down the steps to his sister and helped lift her to a standing position, "Are you harmed, Dicey?" Henry examined her face and arms, checking for cuts or bruises.

"All is well, Henry. I am not harmed. Where are the little ones?"

"They are upstairs. We hid under the bed in my room until the men left. They are still there."

Henry helped Dicey into a chair and then brought her a drink of water from the kitchen. Dicey's heart continued to pound and her breathing grew heavy. "Drink this. It will help calm you."

As Dicey took a sip from the cup, Henry turned toward the front door, shut and bolted it.

"I'm sorry, Henry. They caught me completely off guard. I thought they were the liberty men returning for something."

"They probably saw the others leave and knew it would be a safe time to harass us. Don't vex yourself over it Dicey. There was little you could do," comforted Henry.

"But I didn't have to make it so easy for them! Poor mother! They took all of her good china and silver and that pewter basin that belonged to Grandmother! She will be heartbroken."

"But they did not take her children, Dicey. And you know that will be what mother will care most about."

"You are right about that, Henry. The Lord indeed watched over us this day."

~*~

Within less than an hour, Solomon and Sarah Langston returned to find their home ransacked.

"What in the world happened here?" exclaimed Sarah Langston as she held Dicey's face between her hands and searched her eyes. "Are you harmed? Where are the children?"

"Everyone is safe, Mama. Captain Gray and his men did this. I'm sorry that I allowed this to —"

"Dicey stood bravely before them, Papa. You would have been proud," interjected Henry before Dicey had a chance to confess to her carelessness in allowing them to enter so easily.

Dicey hung her head. She felt so responsible for allowing them in, but she knew in her heart that had she not opened the door, they would have knocked it down.

Amy, Bennett, and Celin came running down the stairs and clung to their mother's skirt. Sarah lifted Amy to her hip and hugged Celin and Bennett with her other arm. "I am so grateful that you are all unharmed!"

Solomon took Amy from her mother's arms and hugged her as Sarah surveyed her home searching for any valuables that may have escaped the thieves' grasp.

"I'm afraid they got everything of value," noted Dicey. "I'm so sorry that I did not stop them!"

Sarah Langston rushed to her daughter and threw her arms around her, "For heaven's sake, Dicey, you aren't invincible. You kept yourself and the children alive and that is what is important."

"I think the good Lord kept us alive. Captain Gray threatened that if he didn't have so much respect for Papa, he would have done us great harm."

"He threatened Dicey's virtue is what he did Papa," interjected Henry, "And he knocked her to the ground."

"Respect! What respect?" Solomon Langston ran his hands through his hair. "If he had an ounce of respect, he wouldn't have vandalized our home or treated my daughter so shamefully. But I am grateful that the hand of the Lord attended you children today and that you kept your wits about you, Dicey!"

"Come with me, Dicey and Celin. Let's prepare dinner and try to get our minds off things," suggested Sarah.

"Henry, come with me to the tool shed and let's see if we can find something to repair the front door. It's barely hanging on its hinge" instructed Solomon.

As Dicey sat at the table peeling potatoes over a bucket, her mind wandered to strapping Thomas Springfield and his eyes that seemed to read her very thoughts. Dicey had never felt this way about any young man. She'd listened to Liz rattle on about Samuel Holton, but never imagined that any man could make her lose her wits enough to act as foolishly as she had today. *They say the Lord protects fools and little children. Today I acted like both! Is this what love is like? If so, it's something I can ill afford!*

Yet, throughout the afternoon and evening, Dicey's thoughts continually turned to Mr. Springfield. *I wonder how old he is? He doesn't look much older than me. I wonder what it's like to be so young and fight in the war? Where is he from? What kind of family does he have? Does he have someone waiting for him back home?*

Dozens of questions paraded through her mind, but the one that returned more than the others persisted, *Will I ever see him again?* She knew he headed for Woods Fort – that's what James had told her the morning he entrusted her with the rifle. Woods Fort wasn't far from where James and his men often camped. This solitary fact gave her hope that one day they might meet again.

As night fell over the Langston home, Dicey settled into her bed and pulled up the covers around her waist. She leaned over to her night table to take one last look at the time before settling in for the night. As she held Grandfather's pocket watch in front of her, it rattled and felt unstable. Heartsick that it might fall apart in her hands at any moment, she quickly studied the watch to determine if it remained intact.

I've never seen this before! It must have jarred loose when I fell today! As she studied the watch, she could see that a facing had become loose inside the front cover of the watch. She loosened it the rest of the way and to her pleasant surprise found a small storage compartment. She hoped perhaps there would be something inside, but it was empty. *I wonder if Grandpa even knew about this? This may come in handy!*

She reassembled the watch and placed it on her night table, extinguished the lantern, and snuggled under her covers, replaying the more pleasant events of the day in her mind as she drifted off to sleep.

Chapter 4

"Now that the breakfast dishes are done, may I go for a ride to visit Beth, Mama?" Dicey hoped her mother could spare her long enough for a visit to her sister-in-law's, "I promised James I'd check in on Beth every now and then."

"Certainly, my dear, I'd go with you, but I have too much sewing to finish today. Send her my love."

"Thank you, Mama. I will!" she gave her mother a quick hug, darted out the kitchen door and headed for the stable.

"Be careful, dear. Stay to the marked paths!" Sarah Langston warned as Dicey closed the door behind her.

Dicey approached Gabriel, extending her right hand to stroke his face, "Hello, my friend. How are you this morning?" Gabriel was a gentle quarter horse with a golden brown coat offset by a beautiful blonde mane. James had given him to her a couple of years earlier and Dicey had come to see him as one of her dearest friends.

She put on his bridle, mounted the saddle on his back and then stepped into the stirrup, pulling herself into the saddle. Dicey never rode sidesaddle; her brothers taught her how to ride as they did. Gently she nudged Gabriel's sides with her feet and took off toward James and Beth's house. They didn't live far, only a mile or two. As instructed, she followed the main roads.

When she arrived, Beth sat outside on her front porch rocking and fanning herself. Beth, an attractive twenty-one-year-old woman with deep brown eyes, arranged her dark brown hair neatly on top of her head in a bun. She wasn't much taller than Dicey. As Dicey started up the road, Beth ceased rocking and waved her fan in the air in a welcoming motion.

"Isn't this weather gorgeous?" Dicey exclaimed as she tied Gabriel to a tree in the front yard.

"Isn't it?" exclaimed Beth as she continued to fan herself. "So what new adventures have you embarked upon lately, Miss Dicey?" asked Beth with a grin spreading from ear to ear.

"Captain Gray and his men looted our house yesterday!"

Beth's smile abruptly turned downward, "Oh my! Were you there when it happened? Was anyone injured?"

"I stayed home with the children while Mama and Papa were in town. They stormed in and took practically everything of value, but they did leave us unharmed, thank the Lord!"

"How completely terrifying for you! You, my dear sister-in-law, get into more scrapes than anyone I know – excepting James possibly."

"Speaking of James, have you seen him lately? How is he?"

"He came home a couple days ago. He's as handsome as ever. He left something for you and asked me to have you give it to the men who are coming to retrieve the rifle."

"They came yesterday!"

"Oh, no! That's not good. He insisted that this important message be delivered as soon as possible. He expected the men to arrive tomorrow and since you would be seeing them sooner than anyone, he thought it best if I kept it here and gave it to you when you came for your usual Tuesday visit," Beth explained with a worrisome expression.

"Then I'll just take it to them. I've got Gabriel with me, I can ride to Woods Fort right away and get back before anyone misses me. Who am I to deliver it to?"

"I believe the man's name is Spring—, Springwell? Spring—

"Springfield?" Dicey finished, biting her lip to hold back the smile that threatened to burst from inside.

"Yes, that's it. I'll go get the message."

"I'll take Gabriel over to the barn for some water while you fetch it."

Beth entered the house while Dicey took Gabriel to a water trough by the barn. The prospect of seeing the tall handsome Lieutenant again sent Dicey's nerves a flutter. She had hoped that they would meet again, but never imagined that it would be so soon.

Shortly, Beth came out of the house holding a small piece of paper in one hand and a cup of water in the other. "Here, Dicey, you've got at least an hour's ride ahead of you; you'll need a drink as well," Beth held out the cup for Dicey to take.

"You're always so thoughtful, Beth! Thank you so much."

As Dicey drank the water, Beth explained about the paper, "James says this message is different than most he's given you. It's encoded. So normally where he'd have you memorize a message and then deliver it, this time, he needs you to carry it on paper. He warned that you should be extra careful and find somewhere to hide it so that if you were caught, it wouldn't be found."

Dicey tied Gabriel to a hitching post, and suggested, "Let's go inside the house away from possible prying eyes. You never know."

The two women walked side-by-side toward the house and then Dicey followed Beth through the doorway. Dicey entered James' study and closed the door behind them. She set her cup down on the desk and took a seat in a high back chair next to its mate in which Beth seated herself.

"Please...let me see it," Dicey extended her hand to receive the paper, "It's not very large and the message itself doesn't take up all of the paper. I have an idea." Dicey began tearing away portions of the paper upon which nothing was written.

"Dicey! Be careful! Why are you tearing it? I don't have another copy."

"I'm being careful. I won't tear any of the writing."

As she finished her task she explained, "See, it's very small now. I can fold it up until it's tiny, and I have just the place for it."

Beth watched intently as Dicey pulled the pocket watch from her apron pocket and opened the front cover, exposing the secret compartment.

"I discovered this only last night. It seems quite Providential that I should find a use for it this morning," she placed the small piece of paper into the watch and fastened back the cover. "See there, Beth, it's a perfect hiding place!"

"That it is! Absolutely perfect!"

"It will be our little secret about the pocket watch, won't it, Beth?"

"Of course! I won't tell a soul."

"Very well, is there anything I can do for you before I go?"

"No, I'm doing just fine. Now you must be on your way. If you hurry, your parents shouldn't notice you being gone longer than a normal visit to my house."

"If for some reason it takes me longer, you will cover for me won't you Beth?"

"Of course, my dear. I'll just tell them that I've been lonely and enjoyed your company so much that I didn't want you to leave," she smiled. "That would be a true statement. I do enjoy your company, and I do not wish for you to leave, but I know you must."

The two women rose to their feet. Beth reached forward and embraced her sister-in-law, "God be with you, my dear."

"And with you, Beth."

Beth stood in the doorway and watched as Dicey mounted Gabriel and rode at full speed toward Woods Fort. She felt it unwise to stay to the main roads this time. She didn't want anyone seeing her, so she rode through a shortcut that James had shown her that took her in the northerly direction that she required.

Her trip passed speedily and without event. As she approached the fort, two guards stopped her, "What is a little lady such as yourself doing out here, Miss Langston?" inquired the jovial, heavy set man who had been at her home only yesterday.

"I have a message for Lieutenant Springfield," she explained.

"You may call him Captain Springfield now, Miss. After his bravery in battle in Lancaster District, he received a promotion upon arriving here at Woods Fort," the man explained.

"That is quite admirable – I - I'm sorry, Sir, but I never caught your name yesterday," Dicey questioned.

"My name is Lieutenant Hammonds, Miss."

Dicey dismounted Gabriel and held the reigns in her left hand as she extended her right to shake his hand, "Nice to see you again, Lieutenant Hammonds. Would you be so kind as to lead me to Captain Springfield, Sir?"

"Of course, Miss. Just follow me." Lieutenant Hammonds signaled to another man to take his post and motioned for Dicey to follow him inside the fort. Dicey entered the structure, leading Gabriel at her side.

"You may tie your horse here, Miss," he pointed to a hitching post just inside the fort. Dicey wrapped the reigns around the post and patted Gabriel on the neck.

The fort's circular structure spanned five hundred feet in diameter and the timber comprising its walls stood about ten feet high. Inside were two small cabins, a watchtower between them, and a dozen neatly placed rows of tents in front. Lieutenant Hammonds led Dicey to the cabin on the right and tapped lightly on the door.

"Yes, who is it?" came a voice from inside.

"It's Lieutenant Hammonds with a messenger for you, Captain Springfield."

"Send him in."

Lieutenant Hammonds opened the door and motioned Dicey to enter, shut the door behind her and left.

Captain Springfield stood with his back to Dicey, thumbing through a stack of papers that lay on his desk, as if he were searching for one document in particular.

"Yes? You have a message for me?" he questioned blandly without raising his head.

Dicey's heart raced, "Yes Sir, I have an encoded message here for you" she began.

Instantly, Captain Springfield turned around to face Dicey, "It's you."

"Yes, it's me." she couldn't help but find humor in his statement. She found the astonished yet pleased expression on his face comical, and a grin started to break forth as she bit her lip to contain it.

"*You* have an encoded message for me?" he asked quizzically.

"Yes, my brother James didn't expect you to arrive at our house until tomorrow and he thought that I would be able to give you this message with the rifle. He left it with his wife who gave it to me today. I thought it best to deliver it myself."

"That's very kind of you."

"It's nothing."

He took a step toward her until they were standing face to face, "So where is this encoded message?"

The excitement of seeing Thomas Springfield again made Dicey completely forget that the encoded message lay hidden within her secret hiding place. It certainly would be unwise to reveal this to another person, but hiding it now would be impossible. Thomas Springfield stood before her and he expected the message. Something told her that if she could trust anyone, she could trust him.

"I – I have it in a safe place."

"Safe as it may be, I will need to see it in order to decode it," he held out his hand to receive it.

"I know. If you will give me a moment, I will give it to you," Dicey stepped closer to the desk and pulled the pocket watch from her apron. Thomas followed her until he stood next to her.

"Please keep this as our secret. I do not wish for anyone else to know of my secret hiding place."

An expression of curiosity pervaded his face, "Certainly, it will be our little secret."

She looked up into his eyes and felt herself getting lost in them. Her heart fluttered nervously. *Get a hold of yourself, Dicey,* she told herself. She shook her head slightly and diverted her gaze back down at the watch as she flipped up the top of it and began opening the compartment. She withdrew the scrap of paper, unfolded it, and pressed it flat on the table to remove the creases. She turned toward Thomas extending the paper to him. "Here it is, Sir."

"Well, isn't that handy!" he marveled.

"It is, isn't it? But please, don't tell anyone about my hiding place. I may need to use it again," she asked as she began reassembling the watch.

"Do you do this kind of thing often?" he inquired as he glanced at the paper.

"My brother often asks me to deliver messages to the Patriots."

Thomas shifted the paper from his right hand to his left and reached out to grasp Dicey's hand. "You are a rare woman, Miss Langston."

He lifted her hand to his lips and kissed it. "Thank you so much for taking the trouble to deliver this message. We are fortunate to have a woman such as you to come to the aid of our country in these perilous times."

"It was nothing, Captain Springfield. I consider it an honor to help the cause of liberty in any way I can. I will do so until my dying breath."

Her statement seemed to catch him off guard, "Do not speak of death, my dear lady. I trust that you will live a long and adventurous life, making one man very happy, and together bless this earth with children as faithful and loyal as yourself."

At the mere thought of Thomas Springfield speaking of her children, Dicey's face grew instantly hot as a crimson glow flushed her cheeks and a honey warm tingle drizzled throughout her body starting at her head and culminating at her toes. Even if he made no implication that he would be the "one man" who would share her life, the thought instantaneously entered her mind and weaved a spell over her like nothing she had ever experienced.

"I've embarrassed you. I'm sorry," he apologized.

"Certainly not. It's rather warm in here, don't you think?" she began fanning herself with her free hand for he still held her right.

"Really? It feels just fine to me" he smiled teasingly.

She knew that he could read her thoughts. There would be no pretending with this man.

"Then again, it can be stifling in here without the breeze. Would you like to step outside and take a tour of the fort?" he asked.

"I really must be going," she stated, but her heart searched for some excuse to stay in his presence.

"Surely you have a moment to look around. I would think you would find it interesting to see a fort since you have played such an important role in our fight for freedom."

Thomas shoved the note into his pocket. He extended his arm to her and Dicey wove her arm through his as he placed his free hand on hers and guided her toward the door.

"Perhaps I have a few minutes to spare," she happily relented.

Dicey and Thomas strolled arm in arm around the fort as he showed her the cannons, the weapons arsenal and the horses.

"And this is the watchtower. We keep a man at the top at all times to search for approaching enemy."

"I'd say you have a wonderful view from up there!" she marveled with her eyes gazing upward.

"Yes we do. Would you like to see it?"

Dicey couldn't resist an opportunity to ascend a watchtower, "I'd love to."

"You'll have to do a bit of climbing. Is that acceptable?"

"Can't be any harder than climbing an apple tree!" she laughed.

"Much simpler," he agreed.

Captain Springfield stood to the left of the ladder and in a gentlemanly-like fashion diverted his gaze until Dicey had reached the top.

"Are you coming up?" she inquired.

"Yes, I just wanted to make sure you arrived at the top first," He turned and began climbing up the ladder. When he reached the top, he gestured to the soldier manning the tower, "Take a little break, Jacob."

Jacob, happy for the rest, smiled and descended the ladder, leaving Dicey and Thomas alone at the top.

Dicey scanned the horizon, "This is absolutely stunning!" she exclaimed. "What a view! You can see for miles around!"

"It's beautiful country around here. I stood here yesterday and a family of cardinals and a blue jay visited me," he related.

If the valiant and handsome Patriot with an endearing sense of humor had not already begun to steal her heart, his appreciation for God's creations alone would have given him access to the deepest reaches of her soul. In an effort to prevent him from discerning her growing interest in him, Dicey approached the railing and leaned over to look down. Instinctively the Captain grabbed her around the waist and pulled her toward him, "Be careful!" he warned.

Dicey spun around to face him, "I'm not going to fall."

"This structure stands out in the weather. It's not exactly the sturdiest thing," he explained, still holding her in his arms.

There were those blue eyes again. They captured her every time she looked into them... as if they were drawing her away to a place from which, if she didn't guard herself, she'd never return. It was a place bathed in heavenly sunlight where time stood still and she could simply reach out her hand and touch eternity.

"May I call on you Miss Langston?" he whispered, still holding her with his hands on her waist and looking into her chocolate brown eyes.

Momentarily taken by surprised, she searched for an appropriate response and decided upon honesty, "Yes, Captain, I would enjoy visiting with you again, Sir."

"You don't need to call me Captain or Sir. Please call me Thomas."

Dicey knew that her mother would be utterly appalled by such a notion. It simply evaded propriety for two people who knew so little of each other to address one another by their given names. But in this moment with his arms encircling her, she really didn't care. She wanted to call him Thomas, but she felt it unwise to appear too eager, "Perhaps some day, Sir," she stepped back from his embrace. "But if at some point I acquiesce and address you by your first name, then you must at that time call me by mine."

"I look forward to that day, Miss Langston."

"I really must be returning home. My family will be worried about me."

"Of course, let me go down first just in case you need some assistance," he suggested.

The Captain descended the ladder and waited for her at the bottom. He made himself ready to assist, but kept his eyes from looking upward until Dicey descended closer to the ground, and then he extended his hand to help her step down from the last few rungs.

He took her arm in his and guided her back to Gabriel. She led the horse by the reins to the entrance of the fort with the Captain at her side. When she started to mount the horse, he turned to her and said, "Thank you again, Miss Langston, for bringing the message."

"You're welcome. Captain – I uh –," she hesitated, unsure whether to verbalize the thoughts that kept running through her mind.

"Yes?" his eyes seemed to beg her to continue.

She decided to be bold, "My birthday is the fourteenth of May and my family has invited a few guests for an afternoon garden party. I would be honored if you were to attend — if you can obtain leave of your duties."

"I will do my very best to be there, Miss Langston. That's a Tuesday, is it not?"

"Yes, two weeks from today."

He helped her climb into the saddle. Atop her quarter horse, she and Thomas were virtually eye-to-eye. He tipped his hat, "Until we meet again, Miss Langston."

She smiled, nudged Gabriel firmly with her heels, "Let's go, Gabriel," and rode away at a gallop. Gabriel carried her through green meadows and babbling brooks and into the forest that bordered Spartanburg and Laurens Districts.

Just as Dicey approached the border of Spartanburg District to go back into Laurens District, she heard the sound of pounding horse hooves crunching leaves and twigs on the forest floor. She urged Gabriel onward at full speed, but the larger horses were no match for Gabriel's shorter legs. Before she knew it horsemen appeared on either side of her, grabbing Gabriel's reins, forcing him to halt abruptly. Dicey fought to regain control, but the loyalist officer on her right pulled her from the horse and held her tightly in his grip. He held one hand over her mouth and the other arm bound her firmly around the waist.

Dicey elbowed the man in the stomach and stomped on
his foot with her heel, sending him doubled over to the
ground holding his stomach with one hand and his foot with
the other. She quickly spun around to run back toward
Gabriel, as another officer stepped in front of her with a pistol
in his hand. Three men now surrounded her: two in front of
her, one of which held a pistol, and the man who had fallen
pulled himself up to stand behind her. Faithful Gabriel
waited nearby within arm's reach. He whinnied and pawed
nervously at the ground, sensing that his mistress was in
danger.

"Miss, we've been following you for some time. We saw
you leave Woods Fort and it will be to your advantage to tell
us what you found there," demanded the man with the
pistol.

"What do you mean, 'what I found there?' I saw men and
horses and a fort."

"No, how many cannons do they have? How many men?
Are they prepared for battle or are they low on munitions?"
the man with the pistol interrogated.

"Why would I know such things? I just went to visit a
friend. Do you think they would give me confidential details
on their readiness for war? Why would a young girl such as I
care for such things?"

"Oh, we know who you are, Miss Langston. Don't pretend
that you are a silly schoolgirl. I believe the Patriots refer to
you as 'Daring Dicey!' Do they not?" grunted the man behind
her who still bent over slightly holding his stomach.

"Most likely you were delivering a message. You will tell
us of your message along with information on the fort's

65

readiness for battle if you wish to live," continued the gunman.

"I will not," she stated resolutely.

The gunman pointed the pistol at her chest, "You will either reveal the information that we require or you shall die in your tracks, Miss Langston."

Dicey replied with the cool and resolute fearlessness of a veteran soldier, "Shoot me if you dare! I will not tell you." As she spoke she opened a long handkerchief lengthwise so that it covered her neck and chest, as if to offer a place to receive the contents of the weapon.

Incensed by her defiance, the officer prepared to fire, when the man next to him threw up his hand to knock the gunman's arm into the air. A shot rang out and the ball lodged into an overhanging tree limb, causing a flock of birds to squawk and take flight from the trees. The surprise of the moment gave Dicey opportunity to grab Gabriel's dangling reins, pull herself atop the animal and ride away at full speed, leaving the loyalist officers to argue among themselves over what had just transpired.

Dicey rode hard all the way home. Knowing that she'd spent too long at the fort and then with the delay from the attack, she dared not stop by Beth's on the way home. She rode straight to the stable, dismounted Gabriel and led him into his stall where she gave him fresh water and food.

"Dicey, you ride that animal entirely too hard," Dicey jumped slightly when she heard her father's voice behind her. She shrugged her shoulders as if it were nothing out of the ordinary, and removed the saddle. "He likes running hard. It's good for him every now and then to work up a good perspiration," she patted the animal dry with a towel.

"Well, it's not ladylike, Dicey. It's time you started acting more like a lady. You'll be fifteen in a couple weeks, and your mother is concerned that you've had too much influence from your brothers to learn the manners of a lady. Personally, I'm in no hurry to marry you off, Dicey. You know how fond I am of having you around, but your mother doesn't want you to waste these prime years. She's concerned about your future happiness."

Dicey closed her eyes and took a deep breath. She could feel the irritation rising within her, but contained it in an effort to show respect for her father. Then an idea struck. Should she say anything? She weighed the options quickly in her mind and decided that it would be better to speak now rather than have her parents play matchmaker for her.

"Papa, mother doesn't need to worry about me becoming a spinster. I promise to act the perfect lady at the party. And if you will keep something between you and me, I have already met someone who will meet with both your approval."

Her father's left eyebrow rose in curiosity, "Indeed? And why is it we have not heard of this young man before now? Who is he?"

"He's a Captain in the Patriot army – someone James introduced to me."

Her father seemed flabbergasted, "When did you meet him? When will *we* meet him?"

"As I said James arranged the introduction recently and he is planning to visit on my birthday if he can obtain leave from the military. You may meet him then. If you will excuse me Papa, I really need to wash up for dinner. I'm dusty from head to toe."

Dicey stepped around her father, leaned up on her tip toes and kissed his cheek affectionately and hurried toward the house, not waiting for his reply. He turned and watched her leave, still reeling from the information she had just shared. He found himself marveling that his tomboyish daughter would be interested in anyone romantically, but of one thing he was certain, he knew he could trust Dicey's judgment. That one fact gave him peace of mind, and he felt rather flattered that she would entrust him with this information.

Chapter 5

As Dicey helped her mother prepare dinner, she replayed the events of the day in her mind. She still trembled slightly and her heart beat a little faster than normal from her close encounter with a bullet on her way home from the fort. What would she have done if one man hadn't taken pity on her? Dicey had learned that if she stood and faced danger head-on, many times it would back down. But she knew that such might not always be the case. There were many in the cause who were not so fortunate and she offered up a prayer of gratitude for the sparing of her life. She entertained no doubt that it was anything other than the intervening hand of Providence by which she was protected.

She thought of the comfort and safety she experienced upon arriving home, finding her father there waiting for her. She still couldn't believe that she told him about Captain Springfield. She and her father were close, but she knew she hadn't been completely honest with him by acting as if Thomas would be the one to save her from a spinster's life. They barely knew each other. She just couldn't stand another minute of all the negative predictions everyone made behind her back. She could still hear her aunt's voice from a few months prior when she didn't realize Dicey stood within earshot, "Poor Dicey, she's a pretty girl, but she's such a tomboy, no man will be interested in her. She'll ever lead a life of loneliness."

Why can't a woman be skilled at hunting, fishing and riding a horse without being a total repulsion to the male population of the earth? Dicey wondered to herself. The mere thought of it made her peel the potatoes with furious strokes, flinging peels left and right, entirely missing the bucket.

"Dicey, dear, your aim is a bit off this afternoon, don't you think?" her mother chuckled as she looked over her shoulder to see peels flying in all directions.

"I'm sorry Mama, I'll be more careful," she muttered as she reached down and picked up the stray peels and placed them in the wooden bucket.

I'm not going to let them get to me anymore, she resolved. Taking deep breaths, she concentrated on getting the peels into the bucket. As she stared at the wooden bucket she thought it resembled the circular wooden fort she had visited earlier in the day. *Just needs a watchtower in the center* she chuckled to herself. She began to replay the events of the morning with Captain Springfield in her mind, and soon a smile spread across her face.

Her mother glanced over her shoulder, and then stopped cooking to turn around and stare at her daughter. Dicey continued to peel, oblivious to her mother's observation.

"What has you in such a chipper mood suddenly, Dicey?" she asked.

"Oh, nothing much, just happy to be here making dinner with you and Celin, Mama," Dicey flattered in a vain attempt to divert her mother's attention.

"We've made hundreds of dinners together, Dicey. Why is this afternoon one that fills you with such gratitude?"

"I'm just feeling happy this afternoon, Mother. Do I need a reason to be happy?"

"No, but only five minutes ago, I would have sworn that you were ready to start a fist fight with those potatoes. Seems quite a shift in your attitude from one moment to the next."

"I just decided to be happy and thought of something pleasant is all," Dicey explained truthfully.

"It's wise of you to recognize that happiness is a choice, my dear," Sarah decided not to press her further. She felt very proud of her daughter, even if her moods over the past couple days could shift from frustration to elation on the flip of a coin. *Perhaps this is a sign that she's learning to control her moods?* Sarah hoped to herself and returned to her work.

Dicey planned her birthday in her mind. *I hope Papa will arrange for music at the party. I'd love the chance to dance with Thomas.* He was no longer "Captain Springfield" in her mind. She had already started calling him "Thomas" in her thoughts; although she resolved to be more formal when speaking aloud. *Only fourteen more days and I'll see him again! But what if he can't get away on a Tuesday? Why didn't we plan my birthday party for a Saturday or a Sunday? Yes, a quiet get-together on Sunday would have been best - less likelihood of a battle on the Sabbath. What if they can't spare Thomas through the week?*

At the very thought that Thomas might be unable to attend, Dicey's countenance fell, and through her peripheral vision, Sarah could see the strips of potato peel sailing through the air.

Then again, perhaps she has not learned to control her moods after all, Sarah chuckled to herself.

~*~

Summer fast approached, and for women in society, this meant airing out mattresses and pillows and sewing cooler dresses and shirts for summer. While Dicey would rather be fishing with Henry, her mother needed her around the house. Sarah Langston instructed her daughters in all the necessary homemaking skills of the day and Dicey possessed adequate seamstress abilities. She spent the remainder of her week busily performing homemaking duties alongside her mother and daydreaming about Thomas, counting the days until she would see him again.

Inside she nearly burst at the seams. She longed for someone to talk to about Thomas but felt awkward telling her mother. While she felt close enough to have confided in her father, she did not feel comfortable discussing details. Liz was the only person with whom she felt willing to share this kind of information and that would have to wait until Sunday after church. They often walked home together and Dicey couldn't wait until she had some private moments with her best friend to confide in her about the man who occupied her thoughts.

Sunday morning arrived and Dicey eagerly dressed for church and helped the little ones get dressed.

"I can't find my Sunday shoes, Dicey. Will you help me?" cried Celin.

"Why can't you ever keep them in your room in their proper place, Celin?" Dicey chided.

"I don't know. I put them there, but they aren't there now!" Celin plopped down on the floor and started to pout.

"Well, you won't find them sitting there on the floor," Dicey laughed. "Come along," Dicey extended her hand to Celin and pulled her to her feet. "We'll find them. Let's start in your room."

Soon the shoes were found – one underneath Celin's bed and one under Amy's. "Let's hurry. We don't want to be late for church," Dicey encouraged as she quickly helped Celin with her shoe.

The rest of the family already waited outside on the buckboard. Dicey lifted Celin into the wagon and climbed up to sit next to Henry.

"You seem chipper this morning, Dicey," Henry observed.

"I'm looking forward to seeing Liz." Dicey admitted.

"I guess Mama has been working you pretty hard. You haven't had a chance to run off to Liz's house all week," he noted.

"Yes, I am most definitely looking forward to my day of rest!" she smiled.

There was only one small church in the neighborhood and the Langston's attended more out of their duty to God than their desire to associate with their fellow church members. Laurens District being primarily Loyalist territory, most of the Langston's neighbors and fellow-churchgoers were Loyalist.

When the fighting started in South Carolina and Dicey's two brothers joined the Patriot forces, the Langston family became the object of ridicule and derision by many prominent members of the congregation. Most of the Patriots in the village stopped attending church because they either felt so unwelcome by the majority of loyalists or held so much animosity for them that they refused to attend.

"We don't attend church to socialize; we go to worship the Lord," Solomon Langston told his family. "We will do our duty to God, fearing not what man may do, loving our enemies and doing good to those who despitefully use us and persecute us. I feel certain that the Lord will bless us for it."

So the Langstons continued to go to the little church on the hill, surrounded by people who disagreed with their political views and who either tolerated or openly persecuted them for those views. But there were a few who were kind irregardless of their stance on the war, like Liz and her family. That spoke volumes to Solomon Langston, and he held Liz and her family in high esteem for their choice to continue to befriend those whom most would consider their "enemies."

As the Langstons approached the church, Liz and her family followed close behind them. Dicey lagged back and waited for Liz to climb out of her family's wagon, and rushed over to greet her.

"Liz! I'm so happy to see you! I have so much to tell you!" Dicey greeted enthusiastically.

"My heavens, Dicey, I don't believe I've ever seen you this excited! What is it?" Liz's enthusiasm bubbled over just from seeing her friend in such a state. "It must be wonderful! You look absolutely radiant!"

"It is wonderfully exciting to me!" Dicey wished she could skip church entirely to chat with her friend, but she knew her father would be furious if she did.

"I can't wait to hear all about it." Liz lowered her voice to a whisper, "Do you think we could slip away and forgo the service? Anything that has you this excited must be incredible!"

"We better not. Let's go in for the services and then walk home together afterward. I'll tell you all about it then," she suggested.

"Why 'Daring Dicey!' you're not daring enough to skip church?" Liz teased.

"I choose my battles wisely and today, with what I have to tell you, you'll see why I want to keep my parents in a good humor," Dicey explained.

"Now you really have my attention. I can hardly wait!" Liz grabbed Dicey's arm and the two hurried into the church.

Dicey and Liz sat down next to each other on a back pew and waited for the meeting to start.

"So give me a little hint," Liz whispered to Dicey, gently nudging Dicey's ribs with her elbow.

"I met someone." Dicey whispered, her eyes darting around to make sure no one could hear.

"You met someone?" Liz looked puzzled for a second, "Oohhhh!" recognition registering on her face, "You met *someone!* How exciting! Who is he? Tell me all about him."

"The introduction came through James. His name is Thomas." Dicey whispered.

The organist started to play the opening hymn and the chorister raised her hands indicating the congregation should stand. Dicey and Liz stood and Dicey began to sing along.

"So Mister Thomas, is he one of the Thomas boys over in Ninety-six District?" Liz searched her memory for any other Thomas families in the area.

"Oh, no," Dicey whispered, "His last name is Springfield. It's Thomas Springfield. He's originally from Granville County, North Carolina," Dicey patted Liz's arm, "I'll tell you all about him on our walk home." The two girls joined in with the song and then sat quietly next to each other through the sermon.

Liz felt grateful for the opportunity to digest this new information. She couldn't believe levelheaded Dicey would fall for anyone. She always thought Dicey beautiful and any man would love to have her as his wife, but somehow this romantic side to Dicey had never surfaced before. She figured Dicey would marry because it made sense, not because she fell head over heels in love. But Dicey appeared to be completely smitten and Liz found it not only out of character but also rather humorous. The mere thought of it forced Liz to bite her lip to keep from giggling aloud.

After the service ended, Dicey and Liz quickly found their parents to let them know that Dicey would be accompanying Liz home. The two girls met at the front door and quickly descended the steps to the pathway leading to the main road.

Dicey suddenly turned to Liz, "Wait, I'm not keeping you from Mr. Holton am I? He's been walking you home the last couple of weeks. Had he planned to escort you today?"

"I didn't notice him at church. So, go on... tell me all about Mr. Springfield! How did you meet? What does he look like? Does he like you too?" Liz bubbled over with questions.

"Slow down!" Dicey laughed. "Now before I tell this story, I want you to promise me that this is just between us. Nobody must know any of this."

"I promise," Liz offered eagerly.

Dicey's face turned very serious, "No I mean it, Liz. There are some parts to this story that must not reach the ears of certain people – especially people your father or Samuel Holton associate with. So do you promise me, Liz? All of this is between you and me – right?"

"I promise. I won't breathe a word of it to a soul." Liz pledged solemnly.

Satisfied that Liz's word was her bond, Dicey began her story. She told her about the rifle and her secret visit to the fort, their moment on the watchtower and inviting Thomas to her birthday party.

"He's attending your birthday party?" Liz inquired excitedly, "So I'll be able to meet him!"

"Yes, that is if he can get away. I hope he can. It may be difficult though since the military may not be able to spare him," Dicey explained.

"So that's one more man in your life for you to agonize over. I'll be so glad when this war is won and we can all stop worrying."

"I've been thinking all week and although Thomas is near where they fought the battle of Musgrove Mill last August, I don't believe he'll see much combat where he is. According to James, most of the battles have moved further north into

North Carolina and there's mainly just skirmishes and neighbors fighting neighbors here in South Carolina. So I'm hoping that Thomas will stay where he is and remain unthreatened."

Beautiful magnolia trees lined the walkway leading into the Williamson plantation. Their dark green leaves and bounteous white blossoms created a canopy over the girls' heads as they strolled toward the house. Suddenly two men stepped out from the foliage and halted in front of them. One had so much dried blood matted to his hair and face that he was nearly unrecognizable. He had both his arms around his companion holding up his limp body. Blood soaked the unconscious man's chest from a gunshot wound in his shoulder.

"Samuel! Is that you?" Liz cried as she ran to Samuel Holton and began stroking his cheek and wiping the blood from his face with her handkerchief.

"Liz, we need your help. We were overtaken by rebels who struck me over the head, shot Matthew and seized our horses," Samuel Holton panted.

"Here, let us help you carry him," Dicey offered. Samuel carried the upper half of Matthew Love's body as Dicey and Liz each took a leg and the three of them carried Mr. Love to the house.

"We can put him in the spare bedroom. There are two small beds in there - one for each of you," Liz planned ahead.

When they reached the guest room they placed Matthew Love in the bed near the window and Liz guided Samuel to the bed near the doorway and instructed him to lie down. "You look horrible Samuel! You've bled so much! Are you in

78

great pain?" fresh tears started rolling down Liz's cheeks as she gently wiped the blood from his face and forehead with her handkerchief.

Dicey sat next to Mr. Love and quickly tore his shirt open to examine the wound, "This looks quite bad, but on the brighter side no one will have to fish for the bullet. It looks like it went clean through the other side of his shoulder. Liz, go put some water on to boil, please"

Liz darted to the kitchen and started a pot of water on the stove. As she stepped back into the room, Dicey turned to her, "Where are your father and mother, Liz? Are they back from church? We could really use their help."

"They were staying after church for choir practice for about an hour. What do you need me to do next?" Liz asked anxiously.

"Let's try to get them as cleaned up as we can and then I'll take one of your father's horses and run for Doc Reid," she explained as she began tearing Mr. Love's shirt completely from his torso and arms to make sure she had found all his wounds. As she lifted his wrist, Dicey's face turned pale.

"What is it, Dicey? You look as if you've seen a ghost," asked Liz. "Is he dead?"

Samuel sat up in his bed and anxiously looked at Matthew. Dicey's face turned from pale to red as she angrily spun around, "Mr. Holton, why didn't you tell us that Mr. Love is a Bloody Scout before you allowed us to bring him into this house?"

Evident shock saturated Liz's face as she turned from Dicey to Mr. Holton and back to Dicey. "What do you mean, Dicey? Why do you think he's a Bloody Scout?" she gasped.

"See here," she held up Mr. Love's wrist, "All the Bloody Scouts wear this serpent's brand on their forearm. So why didn't you tell us, Mr. Holton? You know that Liz's father would be infuriated if he knew a Bloody Scout set foot in his home. He may be Loyalist, but I've heard him say on more than one occasion that the Bloody Scouts were nothing more than murderers and thieves using the war as an excuse to appease their violent lusts for blood and property."

Dumfounded, Liz agreed, "Dicey's right, Samuel. Father will be furious. Why didn't you tell us?"

Then the horror of it struck both the young women simultaneously, and their eyes met knowingly. Only Dicey mustered the courage to verbalize their worst fears, "Mr. Holton, if you are associated with this man, then does that mean you are one of them as well?"

Samuel Holton quickly rolled up his shirtsleeves as he spoke, "No, Liz, I promise you, Darling. I'm not a Bloody Scout!" He showed her his arms, front and back. "I – uh – I mean, Matthew wanted me to join, and I must be truthful and tell you that I considered it, but this very morning I told him that I had decided against it."

"Samuel Holton! How could you even entertain such a notion?" Liz's queried with astonishment.

"I'm sorry, Darling, I am so ashamed to admit that I would even consider it, but you know how desperately I love you and want to marry you. But my family is not as well off as I've led you to believe. In the last year or so, my father has gotten caught up in speculation and has lost our family fortune. We are deeply in debt. I won't be able to provide the type of life you are accustomed to, and that breaks my heart. I

cannot possibly ask you to marry beneath yourself." Samuel
hung his head in shame and then continued, "When
Matthew made the offer for me to join with them, he assured
me that I would have all the money I would ever need to set
up a home and provide for you. And so I agreed to attend one
of their meetings this morning. That's why I didn't go to
church. But as we left, I told him I just couldn't do it. I just
can't steal from other people – even if they are rebels – and
then build my home with their possessions. It's just not
right!"

Liz ran to Samuel and threw her arms about his neck and
kissed his blood stained cheeks, "Oh Samuel! Don't you
know that I would marry you even if we have to live in a one-
room cabin! I love you and nothing else matters." She gently
kissed his lips and smiled through her tears.

"You are too good for me Elizabeth Williamson," he said
as he fell into her embrace.

Dicey gave the pair a minute to collect themselves and
then broke the silence, "So that takes care of you, Mr. Holton.
Now what do we do with this Bloody Scout that lies here?" a
concerned expression furrowed Dicey's brow.

"Matthew may have chosen a wrong path, but he is my
friend, Miss Langston. We've known each other since we
were children. Would you please help him and try to forget
what he represents?" Samuel pleaded.

Dicey weighed the situation and then relented, "Very
well, Mr. Holton. Liz, please fetch that boiling water, a bottle
of whisky and some more bandages, and finish cleaning and
binding up Mr. Holton's head. I'll see what I can do for Mr.
Love."

When Liz returned with the items, Dicey poured some of the boiling water into a basin of cool water and tested the temperature with her fingertip.

"Grab another basin of warm water for Mr. Holton to clean his head while I use this one for Mr. Love," she instructed.

Mr. Love lay completely unconscious as Dicey cleansed the wound with whisky and warm water.

"He still needs a doctor," Dicey turned to Liz, "But we need to hide the fact that he's a Bloody Scout. Doc Reid is no friendlier toward Bloody Scouts than your father is."

"Is there some way to cover it up so no one sees it?" Liz suggested.

"That's a good idea. I'll bandage the arm that has the brand." Dicey agreed.

"But what if the doctor sees the bandage and wants to examine under it?" Samuel questioned.

"We'll have to tell him that it's just a scrape and that I took care of it, but that his shoulder is what needs the attention," Dicey shrugged, "We'll just have to hope he takes my word for it." Dicey stood and prepared to leave. "Liz, I hear your father downstairs. Please tell him that Mr. Holton and Mr. Love were attacked. Have him come up here and stay with you and the men while I go ride for the doctor."

Liz left the room and started down the stairs to find her father.

"You're really going to cover for a Bloody Scout, Miss Langston?" Samuel asked with incredulous astonishment.

"I'm not covering for a Bloody Scout. I'm doing this for my best friend. If her father ever finds out that you were involved

in any way with the Scouts, you'll never be allowed to see Liz
again. There will be no wedding. And I cannot bear to watch
Liz's heart broken. I'm doing this for Liz and for you. I believe
you're a good man, Mr. Holton, and although you may have
been tempted, you did not succumb. And for that you are to
be commended."

Within moments, Liz and her father entered the room.
"My boy, what has happened to you? You look like the
devil!" Mr. Williamson approached Samuel and the tall grey-
haired gentleman shook the younger man's hand.

"I'm going for Doc Reid, Mr. Williamson. May I take one
of your horses?" Dicey asked.

"Certainly, dear, take the black stallion. He's the fastest
you know." Mr. Williamson winked. He knew that Dicey
loved to ride fast and that the stallion was her favorite.

"Thank you, Sir," she grinned and then gave Liz a quick
hug. "Don't worry, my friend, everything will be all right,"
Dicey whispered into Liz's ear. "I'll be back soon."

Dicey ran to the stable, maneuvered a bale of hay next to
the stallion, grabbed his saddle, stood on the hay bale and
threw the saddle over the stallion. Climbing atop the animal,
she nudged his sides with her boot heels and rushed for Doc
Reid's house. The physician only lived about a mile from the
Williamson's so with the stallion running at top speed, she
arrived in a flash. Outside the doctor's house, she quickly
dismounted, tied the stallion to a post and ran to the door.

She knocked loudly and Mrs. Reid answered, "Miss
Langston, what are you doing here?"

"I've come for Doc Reid. A man's been shot and another wounded. They're at the Williamson's. Will you please tell the Doctor I'm here and ask him to come quickly?"

"Why certainly, dear, please step inside," Mrs. Reid moved aside and allowed Dicey to enter, then walked to the doctor's study to inform him.

Dicey heard the doctor's footsteps on the hardwood floor coming from the other room. "Miss Langston, you say there's been a shooting?"

"Yes, Mr. Holton and his friend were attacked this morning and they're at the Williamson's home. Please come quickly."

"Let me grab my bag, I'll be right with you," the doctor stepped back into his study and returned with his medical bag.

"We've cleaned and bandaged them the best we could," Dicey explained. "I'll tell you more as we ride."

Dicey and the doctor mounted their horses and road swiftly back to the Williamson Plantation.

As they walked into the Williamson house and up the stairs Dicey told the doctor, "I've examined Mr. Love's torso thoroughly and other than a small scratch on his forearm, that I bandaged, his shoulder is what clearly needs your expert attention. And of course, Mr. Holton's head wound is quite severe as well."

"Well let's have a look," the doctor walked over to Samuel and shook his hand, "Looks like you boys have been into quite a scrape this morning, Mr. Holton."

"Yes, they caught us by surprise. Got both our horses, and since we were closer to the Williamson's house than anywhere else, I thought it best to seek their help," Mr. Holton explained.

"You are quite fortunate that these two fine ladies were here to assist you. They've done an excellent job in cleaning and bandaging your wound. You'll be just fine. Head wounds always bleed profusely. It's not as bad as it looks."

Liz squeezed Samuel's hand and an expression of relief swept across her porcelain features.

The doctor then turned his attention to Mr. Love. Dicey pulled back the cloth that she had packed around his shoulder. "The bullet went clean through I think," Dicey explained.

"Yes, my dear, it did. How did you clean it?" inquired the doctor.

"I used some boiling water and lowered the temperature with a little cool water and also poured whisky straight into the wound. Fortunately he slept through the whole ordeal."

The doctor nodded with approval.

Matthew Love began to stir, "What happened?" he groaned.

The doctor sat on the edge of Mr. Love's bed while Dicey, Liz, Samuel and Mr. and Mrs. Williamson stood over him. "Matthew, remember you were shot by those men who stole our horses. I brought you here to the Williamson's and Miss Williamson and Miss Langston were kind enough to take care of us both," Samuel explained.

Matthew's eyes roved from one face to the next and then his eyes rested upon Dicey, "You helped me, Miss Langston?" he asked bewilderedly.

"Yes, she did," Samuel answered.

"And she did a fine job of cleaning your wound and stopping the bleeding," Doc Reid added.

"I am indebted to you then, Miss Langston." He turned to Liz, "and you too, Miss Williamson."

"Let me just dress this wound a little bit more here, Mr. Love, and within a few weeks you'll be as good as new," the Doctor explained, "Mr. Williamson, it would be best if he isn't moved for a few days. Will you allow him to stay here and perhaps your servants can keep an eye on him? I'll come back to check on him each day over the next few days to make sure he's healing properly."

"That will be fine," answered Mr. Williamson generously.

Dicey turned to Liz, "I think I've done all I can do here, Liz. I'll be returning home now."

"Let me walk you to the door," Liz squeezed Samuel's hand and whispered, "I'll be right back."

The two young women walked down the stairs, out the front door and onto the porch. Dicey turned to Liz and whispered, "Be careful, Liz. Stay away from Mr. Love and let the servants take care of him."

"I will, Dicey. Thank you for helping Samuel and me. Samuel told me what you said about covering for us. You are the best friend a girl could have," Liz embraced her friend and then let her go.

"I'll try to stop by in a few days to see how you are doing." Dicey descended the porch steps, turned to wave goodbye and left for home.

Chapter 6

James Langston reclined against the cold stability of the
limestone boulder as he sat on the ground with his long legs
bent in front of him, the soles of his boots braced against the
ground. His muscular forearms rested on his knees as he
held a green willow limb with a strip of rabbit meat laced
around the end of it over the crackling fire. The warmth from
the embers penetrated the cool spring evening offering a
comforting security in spite of the dangerous mission on
which he was about to embark the next morning.

As the flickering light danced in James' emerald green
eyes, he remembered the first night he spent with his wife in
their log home. He'd built it himself and he replayed the
moment he carried her across the threshold, pride swelling
within him for not only the completion of their homestead but
more importantly for the bride he brought home to dwell in it.
By the time the wedding festivities at his parent's home had
ended, the weather had turned cool so James built a roaring
fire to keep them warm.

He and Beth had been friends for a year before he finally
mustered the courage to court her. He waited until he knew
he could properly provide for her and the family that he

wanted to raise with her. James was nineteen and Beth only sixteen when they married. He had just enlisted in the military for the Patriot cause and spent only a few short days with her before leaving for duty.

His thoughts consumed in the yellow and orange flames, James pondered on his relationship with Beth which had only grown deeper with time. The children they had hoped to have together had never arrived, but they knew that once the war ended and they had more than scattered stolen moments with one another, that would change. For a fleeting instant he could feel her in his arms as they sat before the hearth and warmed themselves in its glow. He could almost hear the melody of her voice, feel the softness of her skin and smell the sweetness of her hair. A bittersweet ache congealed as a lump in his throat when suddenly a cracking twig jolted him from his reverie. His head jerked toward the sound where he saw Captain Thomas Springfield who had just exited from his cabin to join James at the fire.

"Sorry to startle you, Langston," Thomas stepped toward the fire and stood with his right boot balanced atop a rock near the flame. The smoke rose and encircled his head just before a gust of wind blew it aside.

"Want something to eat?" James extended the willow toward Thomas, the rabbit meat dangling from it.

Thomas reached forward and pulled a portion of the meat from the limb, "Thank you!" Thomas put the piece in his mouth and sat down on a flat boulder next to James. The tip of Thomas's boot shuffled nervously in the dirt as he pondered upon whether to venture into a personal conversation with his associate.

"Something on your mind, Captain?" James took a bite of meat and extended the willow to Thomas for him to take another piece.

Thomas reached forward and pulled off another bite, "I've twice had the occasion to meet your sister and was wondering if you might tell me a little more about her?"

A knowing grin stole across James' handsome face, "Ah, you fancy my sister, Dicey, do you?"

"I didn't say that. She just seems to be an unusual young woman and I'm curious about her is all," Thomas kicked nervously at a pebble at his right boot.

"Oh, I see," James bit his lip to keep from smiling. "So what do you want to know about her?"

Thomas couldn't decide what to ask. He wanted to know what made her so brave, whether she had a beau, and what she enjoyed doing when she wasn't brandishing a rifle and delivering secret messages in her pocket watch. He finally settled on something less personal, "How long has she been helping the Patriot cause?"

"The first time was a couple years ago when she was thirteen. She overheard Tories planning to break into a neighbor's home and she told Papa about it. He was still recovering from his battle wounds at the time so he sent Dicey to warn the neighbor of the impending danger. The neighbor was able to hide his belongings and evacuate his family before they arrived."

"Your father must be very proud of her," Thomas observed.

"He is. We all are. She's a remarkable young woman," James nodded. "She's not called 'Daring Dicey' for nothing.

She's carried messages to me on many occasions – everything from the location of troops, to their plans of attack and only last month she saved an entire settlement."

"Really? How did she do that?" Thomas, enthralled by anything he could learn about the young woman, leaned forward resting his elbows on his knees and his chin on his hands. He listened intently as James related Dicey's midnight excursion across the rushing, swollen Tyger River to save the Elder Settlement.

After listening to James relate the adventure, Thomas asked, "So is everyone in your family involved in the cause?"

"Our father fought until he was wounded. He now gets around with a cane. My brother Solomon and I are enlisted, but the others besides Dicey are too young.

"How many children are in your family?" Thomas asked.

"There are seven of us. I'm the eldest. Then there's Solomon, then Dicey, then Henry, Celin, Bennett and little Amy."

"So are you and Dicey close?"

"Very much so. I gave her Gabriel, taught her how to ride and how to shoot. There's not much Dicey can't do," James offered proudly. "What about you? Tell me about your family."

Thomas hesitated, "Oh, there's not much to tell."

"Sure there is, I told you about mine," he prodded jovially. "It's your turn."

Thomas' gaze fell to his feet as he laced his fingers through his hair, leaning his head on his right hand, "I'm an orphan. My parents died when I was two. I'm the youngest

and have two brothers and a sister – Aaron, Moses and
Elizabeth, but I've been on my own now for several years."

"I'm so sorry, Captain, I didn't realize," James shook his
head and diverted his eyes toward the fire.

"It's all right, it's made me a stronger person than I
would have been otherwise, I'd imagine. I am happy with my
life," Thomas nodded and forced a smile to cover the
underlying pain which still remained within him. The need
to divert attention from his own life bolstered Thomas'
courage to proceed in his questions regarding Dicey. "So has
your sister always been so brave?"

James chuckled, "Hmmm.. not always I suppose. I think
her bravery emerged after a bull almost impaled her when
she was eight."

"A bull almost impaled her?" Thomas's blue eyes
widened in astonishment.

James shook his head affirmatively but appeared to have
no intention of relating the story.

"Go on... aren't you going to tell me what happened?"

James shook his head negatively, "Dicey would be
furious if I did."

"Please... continue. I won't tell her you told me," Thomas
prodded.

"You promise? Because she really despises for me to tell
this story."

"I promise, I won't tell her that you told me."

"Very well," James set down the willow and rubbed his
hands together in front of the fire as he prepared to share
what Dicey considered to be one of her most embarrassing
moments. "Dicey was eight years old. Oh, my, she was a cute

little girl! All pigtails and skinned knees, and always getting into one thing or another. On this particular spring morning, she was in a hurry to get to the barn to see the new puppies that had been born during the night. So she decided to take a short cut through the bull pen."

"Oh no," Thomas' eyes widened.

"Yes, well," James chuckled. "The bull caught sight of her and started charging, his nostrils flaring vehemently. She ran as fast as she could, the tromping of hooves pounding relentlessly behind her until she reached the fence. When she had climbed onto the first rung she simply froze. I mean to tell you she just stopped!" James began to chuckle with the memory of it. "She just stood there on the fence bracing herself to take the horns in her rear. As if she could stand there, be tough and take it. She says that she doesn't know what made her freeze up like that, but fortunately I was nearby and snatched her over the fence just before the bull would have gored her in the rear end! From that day forward, she's never turned her back to any danger, but always turns and faces it head on."

"A defining moment then?" Thomas suggested.

"Yes, exactly, a defining moment," James smiled.

~*~

The days leading up to Dicey's birthday were busy with cooking, cleaning, and sewing. The day that Captain Gray and his men ransacked the Langston's home, Sarah had been in town purchasing a bolt of lovely blue material to make a birthday dress for Dicey. Sarah had not mentioned it to her.

She wanted to surprise her daughter with the completed
dress, and spent many late nights in her sewing room
working by glow of a lantern to complete the project.

Monday night before the party, Dicey prepared to retire for
the evening when she heard a knock at her bedroom door.

"Yes, who is it?" Dicey inquired as she stood in her
nightgown, fluffing the feather pillow on her bed.

"It's Mama," Sarah answered through the door.

"Oh, come in, Mama," Dicey welcomed.

Her mother slowly opened the door, holding in her arms
an exquisite blue silk bodice with a low-scooped, heart-
shaped neckline and a matching skirt. Dicey's eyes widened
with delight.

"I made this for you to wear tomorrow for your party,
Dicey," Sarah pleased to see the elation on her daughter's
face, couldn't contain a smile.

Dicey ran to her mother, threw her arms around her neck
and exclaimed, "Oh Mama! It's absolutely stunning! Thank
you so much! When did you have time to make it?"

"I worked on it a little here and a little there. I'm happy
you're pleased."

"How could I not be?" Dicey quickly took the dress from
her mother and held it up to her body, pressing her arm to
hold it to her waist.

"Mama, it's the prettiest thing I've ever seen!" Dicey
already felt so excited and nervous about the events that she
hoped would transpire the following day that she nearly
burst with emotion before her mother had even entered the
room. Now, after seeing the results of her mother's hard work
and her profound expression of love in the form of this

elegant gift, Dicey could no longer contain her emotions or secrets.

"Mama, I *have* to tell you something," she blurted out with a broad smile across her mouth and eyes.

Sarah's eyebrows rose, "It sounds exciting!"

"It is!" she answered.

"Well, tell me, dear!" Sarah's curiosity erupted. She hoped that Dicey's revelation would give her some insights into her daughter's recent shifts in moods and deep reveries.

Dicey grabbed her mother's hand and led her to sit next to her on her bed. Dicey neatly folded the dress on her lap as she turned sideways to address her mother who faced her.

"Mama, I cannot thank you enough for this! I wondered what I would wear tomorrow, because it's a very special day for me – and not just because it's my birthday. I met a young man a few weeks ago who stopped by the house to retrieve a rifle James had left for him. It was the day that Captain Gray ransacked the house – only before that. His name is Captain Thomas Springfield and he's stationed at Woods Fort."

Sarah Langston's eyes widened. Now things were starting to make sense!

"Oh Mama, he is just so handsome! And a perfect gentleman and I just can't stop thinking about him."

Sarah Langston thrilled for her daughter. Finally Dicey showed some sign of snapping out of her tomboy ways and preparing for womanhood.

"There's one other thing I have to tell you and I hope you won't be angry with me." Dicey searched her mother's eyes hoping she could trust her with her secrets, "Please don't tell Papa."

Sarah Langston's eyes furrowed with concern.

"Please Mama, I want to tell you this part, but Papa can't know it."

Against her better judgment Sarah Langston relented, "All right, Dicey. It's our secret." Sarah Langston felt proud and elated that her daughter would be willing to share her secrets with her. Usually she confided in her father.

"I know Papa has told me not to carry any more messages for James, but the day after I met Captain Springfield, I visited Beth and she said that James had a message for Captain Springfield that should have been delivered with the rifle, but he had arrived before they could get it to me. I just had to see him again, Mama! So I rode to Woods Fort and carried him James' message."

Sarah Langston's eyes rippled with worry.

"Don't fret. As you can see, I'm here alive and well to tell the tale," Dicey chuckled. "I delivered the message to him, and then he took me on a tour of the fort and he asked if he could call on me. So I invited him to my party tomorrow. He said he'd try to be here if he could get away. Ever since then, one minute my heart will be reeling from delight that he'll be able to attend, to the next minute fearing that he won't be able to break away from the war. I'm sorry my behavior has been so flighty of late, but now perhaps you will understand why."

Sarah Langston threw her arms around her daughter, "My Dicey's in love!" she stated melodramatically, "It all makes sense now!"

"Oh mother, I don't know that I'm in *love*. Seems a bit strong of a word to use with someone I barely know."

"It doesn't take that long, Dicey." Sarah pulled away from her daughter, holding her with a hand on each shoulder and looking into her love struck eyes. "You've got a good sense of discernment. Trust your feelings," Sarah advised.

"I'm so glad I confided in you, Mama," Dicey gave her mother a quick hug and leapt to her feet holding the bodice and skirt to her once more, "I can't wait to wear it!"

Sarah rose and headed for the door. "You better get some rest, Dicey. Tomorrow is a big day. And don't worry; I'm sure your Captain will be here," she winked.

Dicey turned to watch her mother walk out the door.

"Sweet dreams, Dicey," she called as she closed the door behind her.

Dicey began to dance around the room, holding her dress to her as she did.

"Sleep?" she questioned aloud, "Who in the world could sleep now?"

~*~

Nervous butterflies bounced around in Dicey's stomach as she awoke the next morning, quickly dressed, and ran downstairs to cook breakfast for the family. The entire time she worked, she kept envisioning herself in her new blue dress, dancing with Thomas. Anytime a dark cloud of doubt floated through her mind, she quickly pushed it aside and held the vision of him entering their home and dancing the minuet with her in the large ballroom on the east side of the plantation house.

Wealthy Solomon Langston gave monetarily, emotionally, and physically to the cause of freedom. He didn't believe in flaunting one's wealth, but they did have a large and spacious home. In the days before the war erupted in South Carolina, he and Sarah entertained quite frequently, but things had been more solemn since. This made Dicey's birthday party an even brighter occasion since it had been so long since they had celebrated with friends and family in their home.

Sarah Langston gathered her household servants around her to help with the day's festivities. Soon the kitchen filled with chatter and the sights and smells of pies, cakes and bread baking. Much had been prepared the day before, but there still remained work to be completed this Tuesday morning.

Henry set to work in the ballroom, decorating a large table and the walls with streamers and colored paper. Dicey tried to help her mother in the kitchen, but Sarah insisted, "No, my dear, this is your big day; you go spend some time on your hair and dress. We don't want you getting all steamed up and perspiring working in here." Sarah guided her daughter out of the kitchen into the hallway.

About that time Dicey heard a knock at the front door and crossed quickly to open it widely, "Liz! I'm so happy you came early!" Dicey exclaimed as she threw her arms around her friend.

Dicey still wore her work clothes from preparing breakfast. Liz's eyes traveled up and down Dicey's petite body, but she said nothing.

Dicey pushed her friend's shoulder and laughed, "Don't worry, Liz, I'm not wearing this old thing. I'm waiting until the last minute to get ready so that my new dress stays fresh and clean."

Liz laughed, "Oh, well that's a good idea. But don't wait too long. We want you looking your best when Captain Springfield arrives!"

"Come upstairs with me and I'll show you the gorgeous dress mother made for me," Dicey threw her arm around her friend's shoulders and they both ascended the staircase.

"My word, Dicey! It's the prettiest thing I've ever seen!" Liz exclaimed. "Let's get your hair done and put you in it!"

Liz guided Dicey over to a chair and pushed her shoulders to set her down. "Let's see here, you simply must look stunning for Captain Springfield." Liz grabbed Dicey's hairbrush, let down her wavy, thick chestnut hair and began brushing it. Liz wove Dicey's locks into a beautiful French braid, stood in front of her to loosen a few strands from the front and curled them around her finger to accentuate her heart shaped face with a few ringlets.

"You look beautiful, Dicey! I can't wait to see you in that dress. Put it on!"

Dicey stepped out of her work dress and pulled a corset from her dresser drawer, "Can you please help me with this stay?" Dicey asked her friend. "Pull it as tight as you can, but leave me a bit of room to breathe," she chuckled.

Liz helped Dicey pull the corset tightly, fastened it and then reached for the blue Pierrot bodice. "Lift your arms."

Dicey raised her arms to place them into the three-quarter length sleeves and Liz slipped the bodice over her head, being careful not to disturb her hair.

Liz pulled the silk cords that laced through the front eyehooks of the bodice and tied them tightly. Dicey then slipped in the skirt and fastened it about her waist over her petticoats. "It's a perfect fit, Dicey! You look gorgeous!" Liz quickly grabbed Dicey's looking glass and held it up for her to see.

"Well, I don't look like I just rode five hard miles on Gabriel, do I?" she chuckled and looked up at her friend.

"You certainly do not! Your mother did a fine job, Dicey. It's a perfect shade of blue to accentuate your hair and eyes and the stitches are so meticulous!" Liz studied the seams on the sleeves admiringly.

"Mother is an excellent seamstress, that's for sure."

Liz nodded in agreement, "Captain Springfield won't be able to keep his eyes off of you." she stated matter-of-factly.

Dicey giggled, "That's what I'm hoping for! Oh – I hope he will attend!" she added with a hint of pain in her eyes.

Liz took her by the shoulders, looking her squarely in her chocolate brown eyes, "He'll be here Dicey. You can feel that, can't you?"

"Yes, I believe I can."

The girls could hear guests beginning to arrive. Dicey and Liz descended the stairs and started to greet guests. There were aunts, uncles, cousins and friends. There were young people from the village and even a few from church. Samuel Holton arrived shortly and carried Liz's attention away.

Dicey's stomach churned in nervous knots. As time passed, she started to wonder if Thomas would be there. Dicey milled around talking with people and tried to keep her mind off him, but to no avail.

She looked over to see her father open the door and James and Beth step through the entryway. Dicey ran to the door and threw her arms around her brother's neck, "James, I wasn't sure you'd be able to come! I'm so glad you're here!" she raved excitedly. She turned to Beth, hugged her neck and kissed her on the cheek.

"James and I brought something special for you," Beth leaned forward to whisper in her ear and then turned to look toward the door.

There behind James, stood Thomas Springfield who had just stepped up onto the porch behind them. James and Beth moved aside to allow Thomas to enter. Dicey gazed up into his eyes for a moment, a broad dimpled grin gracing her complexion and a blush of hot pink flushing her cheeks.

On the other side of the parlor, Liz elbowed Samuel's ribs, "Look Samuel, it must be Dicey's beau. Her cheeks are as red as cherries," she giggled.

Thomas removed his hat and hung it on a hat rack by the door. Dicey extended her hand toward him, "I'm delighted you were able to attend, Captain Springfield" she greeted with as much composure as she could muster.

"Thank you for inviting me, Miss Dicey." His eyes traveled up and down the length of her dress, "You – you look absolutely breath taking" he took her hand and kissed it, never breaking eye contact as he did.

The warmth from her cheeks sent a thrilling sensation throughout her body as his lips softly met her fingertips. Dicey's heart pounded more violently now than it did the day she faced Captain Gray and his men. She hoped it didn't drum so loudly that people could hear.

"Do come in, Captain."

He turned toward the left to enter through the open double doors leading into the ballroom where her mother had spread a large table of food and guests lined the walls sitting and standing, laughing and talking with each other. He extended his right arm to her, and she took it as he escorted her into the ballroom.

Thomas placed his left hand on her hand, "You certainly have a beautiful spacious home," His blue eyes surveyed the large ballroom, "I didn't see this ballroom the last time I was here. The doors were closed."

"That's right, they were," she couldn't think of anything more profound to say. Just having his hand on hers made her mind go completely blank.

From across the ballroom, Dicey spied her mother busily carrying a tray of bread from the kitchen to the buffet table. As she turned to return to the kitchen, Dicey and Thomas caught her eye, and she smiled, turning toward them.

"Dicey, won't you introduce me to your friend," she looked up at Thomas, "I don't believe we've met, Sir."

"No ma'am we haven't." he smiled.

"Captain Springfield, this is my mother, Sarah Langston. Mother, this is Captain Thomas Springfield. He's stationed at Woods Fort. He came with James and Beth."

Thomas took Sarah's hand and bowed slightly toward her in greeting, "Nice to meet you, Captain Springfield, I've heard good things about you," she winked at Dicey.

Please, Mother! Can you please be a little less obvious? Dicey scolded her mother in her thoughts.

Thomas looked down at Dicey whose face grew even more crimson than before. He smiled knowingly and turned back to Sarah, "Thank you Mrs. Langston. You have a beautiful daughter and I'm happy I could be here for her birthday."

Sarah touched Dicey's hand that had found its way back around Thomas's right arm, "You two enjoy yourselves. Papa hired a dance master who should be here soon. I must be running back to the kitchen."

As she left, Thomas remarked to Dicey, "You have your mother's eyes. Only yours are even more striking."

"You flatter me too much," Dicey blushed and placed her small hand on her bosom. *He's going to think I'm a tomato* she thought to herself as she could feel the blood rushing to her face yet again.

He leaned over and whispered in her ear, "You're absolutely adorable when you do that."

"Do what?"

"Blush" he chuckled.

Dicey rolled her eyes, *Oh stop it!* She could feel herself blushing again and stamped her foot in frustration.

Thomas held his left hand to his stomach, threw his head back and chuckled heartily. His mirth was contagious and Dicey soon found herself giggling as well.

Liz and Samuel approached them, "So what's so funny?" Liz questioned, a broad smile gracing her beautiful face as her eyes darted from Dicey to Thomas and back to Dicey.

"Oh nothing," Dicey settled down enough to answer.

"Captain Springfield, this is my best friend Elizabeth Williamson and her friend Samuel Holton."

The Captain greeted Dicey's friends and then turned to see the dance master and his band enter through the veranda and begin setting up their instruments in the ballroom.

"Oh, your father hired musicians!" Liz exclaimed excitedly. "How delightful!"

The noise of musicians tuning their instruments and people chatting over the warm-up increased until it became hard to communicate without speaking loudly. Dicey didn't want the world hearing her conversation with Thomas, so she suggested, "Would you like to get a plate of food and sit outside while the musicians prepare to play?"

"That sounds like a fine idea," he agreed and they went to the buffet table and prepared their plates of food with breads, chicken and fresh vegetables along with cups of punch. Thomas followed Dicey out the back door and onto the veranda. A group of people sat outside, so she suggested, "Follow me, I know a quiet spot."

Thomas continued to accompany Dicey until she led him under a large weeping willow tree that stood about a hundred yards from the house and overlooked a duck pond. "I just love sitting under this weeping willow and watching the ducks and swans. It's so cool and shady here," she explained as she sat on a bench under the tree and motioned for him to join her. "Mama saw me sitting under this tree so much, that she made Papa put a bench here for me. She got tired of washing the grass stains out of my clothes, I suspect," she chuckled.

He smiled at her, totally enamored by her ability to be so down-to-earth and yet so graceful and breathtaking at the same time. He forced his eyes to stop staring at her and began eating the food on his plate.

Dicey felt too excited to eat much. She took only a few bites, sipped her drink and then placed the cup and plate on the grass beneath the bench. She turned sideways to face Thomas and asked, "So tell me about how you came to be a Captain at such a young age."

Thomas raised his eyebrows as he hurried to chew and swallow a large piece of bread. He took a sip of his punch to wash it down and then shook his head and tried to avoid her question, "Oh it was nothing, really."

"I think it must have been something! Lieutenant Hammonds said your bravery in Lancaster District earned you the promotion. Please tell me about it."

Thomas Springfield wasn't the type of man to brag, and he felt uncomfortable telling this story to Dicey since he had heard much about her adventures from her brother and felt her bravery far exceeded his own, "Oh, it was really nothing, Miss Langston."

"Please Thomas, please tell me," her eyes pleaded with him.

Stunned that she would call him by his first name, Thomas took courage and began, "We were in Lancaster. The Tories came upon us one morning as we slept. They caught us so unaware that they slew a dozen of our men in their

sleep. I awoke when the man next to me screamed out as a
Tory ran him through with his blade. He came at me next, but
I always sleep on my sword so I pulled it from along my side
and lifted it to block the man's stroke. I yelled for the others to
awake and quickly rose to my feet and started dueling with
my attacker. He cut a gash on my cheek. The scar is still
here," he pointed to his cheek where Dicey had observed his
wound weeks earlier.

"I eventually – uh – took care of him and moved on to the
next man who had our Captain pinned to a tree and
prepared to slay him. I ran up to the assailant and began
dueling with him. To make a long story short, in all that
morning I personally disposed of eight Tories. My Captain
was so grateful that he recommended me for a promotion. So
when I arrived at Woods Fort, they promoted me to Captain
and second in command.

"You definitely earned that promotion!" Dicey was
impressed, and she wasn't easily impressed.

Thomas took another sip of his drink, set his dishes down
on the grass beside him and then in an effort to turn the
conversation stated, "James tells me that you saved the Elder
Settlement."

"Oh, it was nothing," she blushed.

"Sounds like we're a couple of do-nothin's," Thomas
chuckled, rubbed his stomach and leaned his head back to
rest on the back of the bench as he stretched his long legs out
in front of him.

Dicey loved the way he leaned his head back and rubbed
his belly when he laughed. She stared at him as he closed his
eyes, resting them for a moment. She then gave into the urge

that had struck her the first time she met him and tenderly
ran her finger across his scarred cheek.

Thomas' eyes opened suddenly as he turned to look at her
"Did it hurt terribly?" she asked.

"You know, I didn't even feel it. When you're in the
middle of fighting like that, your blood gets to pumping so
fast, you just don't register as much pain I guess. I did wince
a might afterwards when they sewed it up."

The band began to play a reel inside the ballroom. Dicey
hopped to her feet and tugged Thomas' hand, "Come on, I
love a good reel."

Thomas sprang to his feet. *This girl's refreshing,* he thought
to himself. She didn't play games and he felt incredibly
comfortable with her.

"Sounds like fun to me," he held her hand as they strolled
toward the house and entered in the door of the ballroom off
the veranda.

The dancers formed lines of three couples each around the
room. Dicey and Thomas joined the line with two other
couples that included Liz, Samuel, James and Beth. The
couples formed two lines. As the music started all the
dancers advanced then retired and Dicey executed the reel
with Thomas and then with Samuel as the couples weaved in
and out to continue the figure to the end of the room. The
lively rhythm of the music continued as the couples repeated
their enthusiastic dance.

The music stopped, and everyone cheered and clapped.
Thomas headed for Dicey as the musicians began to play a
slower minuet, "May I have this dance, Dicey?"

She thrilled at the sound of him addressing her by her first name, but she wondered what had brought on this familiarity. As he took her in his arms, he read the puzzlement on her face, leaned over and whispered in her ear, "You did say that if you ever acquiesce and call me by my first name, that I should then address you by yours."

As she felt his breath on her neck, goose bumps prickled over her body from head to toe. She pulled back slightly to study his eyes, "And when did I do that?"

"Just outside, you called me Thomas" a twinkle catching his eye as he now understood that she didn't even realize she'd called him by his first name.

Dicey searched her memory, "I did? I'm sorry for being so forward."

"Nonsense, and now that it's done, please continue to call me Thomas or Tom if you'd prefer," he couldn't take his eyes off her for he could hardly believe that she showed an interest in him. How could this daring, lively, beautiful and confident young woman be interested a plain and simple farm boy who'd joined the war to fight for his country? Yet, here he danced with what he believed to be the most beautiful, brilliant and brave woman in all of South Carolina.

Thomas and Dicey danced several more reels and minuets and then stopped for some refreshment. As they filled their cups with punch, Dicey gazed up at Thomas, "Would you like to take a stroll by the pond?"

Thomas used his shirt sleeve to wipe the beads of perspiration from his forehead which had formed from the exertion of so much dancing, "Yes, please." He nodded affirmatively, glad for the diversion.

He filled his cup a second time, gulped it down and then set it next to Dicey's cup. Extending his arm, the pair strolled out onto the veranda and toward the pond.

Solomon Langston, standing beside his wife, watched the couple exit together, "How much do you know about this Captain Springfield?"

Sarah leaned over to her husband. He inclined his ear as she spoke softly, "James thinks a lot of him. He's a decorated Patriot and…" she hesitated then continued, "I think our Dicey's falling in love with him."

Solomon's eyebrows rose in curiosity, "You think it's that serious?"

Sarah nodded her head, "Yes, I do. Can't you see it in their eyes when they look at one another?"

"Hmm…" Solomon didn't know if he liked the idea.

Sarah turned to examine her husband's expression. "Something wrong, dear?" she knew her husband well enough to know when he felt unsettled about something.

"Ever since I heard his name earlier, I've been trying to place it. It sounds familiar to me, but I can't quite lay my finger on where I've heard it before," Solomon scratched his head pensively.

"Why does that worry you so?"

"I don't know, but something about the name, Thomas Springfield, unearths ominous feelings within me," Solomon continued to watch his daughter stroll away with the Captain.

"But he seems like such a fine young man," Sarah shook her head. "And Dicey's an excellent judge of character." Her brown eyes smiled at her husband.

"Yet, I can't help this feeling of dread."

"It's because you're so close to Dicey and you hate to see her leave the nest," Sarah deduced.

"Perhaps… yet…" Solomon decided to hold his peace for now. Maybe he'd remember what it was that troubled him about the name Thomas Springfield.

A pebbled pathway encircled the large pond and a cool May breeze wafted off the water, "This breeze sure feels good after all that exertion," Dicey commented.

"Uh hum, I'm plum tuckered out from all that," Thomas plopped down on a plush grassy spot on the far side of the pond. The barn stood between the couple and the house so that they had a perfect view of the pond and the apple orchards that extended beyond. Only the outer outline of the plantation house remained visible from their location.

Thomas patted a spot of grass next to him indicating that she should sit beside him, "Let's rest for a spell."

Dicey normally would have just plopped down next to him, but today, with her new dress, she wanted to make sure that she took great care to avoid grass stains. So she very gracefully sat next to Thomas making sure that she protected her dress in the process.

He casually reached over and grabbed her small hand and held it in both of his, "You have such tiny hands, Dicey," he mumbled as he stretched out his fingers and held her small hand inside his sizeable palm to compare the two.

Thomas' six-foot, broad shouldered, muscular frame made Dicey's tiny body seem petite in contrast.

He laced his fingers through hers and continued to hold her hand as he turned to face her. For several moments they stared silently into each other's eyes. Dicey wished this day would never end and that he would stay with her always. As if to read her thoughts, he reached up with his free hand and brushed a stray ringlet of hair to the side and cradled her face in the palm of his hand, gently caressing her cheek with his thumb, "You are the most amazing, beautiful woman I've ever met, Dicey." His eyes seemed to drink sweet liquid from her very soul as if he were endeavoring to quench a deep and painful thirst. Slowly his head descended towards hers and he kissed her lips gently. Then as if upon the first taste of a sweet refreshment and finding himself thirsting for more, he kissed her again firmly and passionately.

Dicey's heart pounded and butterflies fluttered within her stomach. She found herself holding her breath as she lost herself in his kiss and ran her fingers through the golden waves of his hair. His hands had moved to her tiny waist where he held her tightly. Reluctantly, he broke from her lips and leaned his forehead momentarily on hers; breathing deeply as Dicey lowered her hand from his hair to rest upon his strongly chiseled cheek. After a moment, he searched her eyes and then rose to his feet, extending his hand to help her rise from the ground.

Dicey took his hand and stood facing him, "I guess we better get back to the party."

"Yes, I suppose so," he mumbled as he bent over and kissed her lips once more. He wanted to stay with her, to relish in her embrace a little longer, but he knew if he did, he would never be able to leave. He had responsibilities to attend to requiring that he return before it grew dark.

"Look – isn't that gorgeous," Dicey pointed with her eyes toward a stunning sunset in the western sky. Thomas, still clutching her hand, turned to imbibe the evening display that burst open with the most remarkable sweeping strains of reds, purples, pinks and blues as the sun set behind the hills.

The pair watched silently as the sun sank and the colors began to subside. Thomas turned to her, "I must leave now," he muttered.

Her heart sank. Couldn't he stay a little longer? Dicey had never been one to cling to anything or anyone for security, but at this moment, she felt that if he left her, her heart would rip apart and leave her utterly abandoned and alone. For once in her life she felt complete, as if she'd found a part of herself that she never knew had been missing until she met this tall, handsome blue-eyed soldier. Could she go back to being only half a person after this perfect day – after experiencing the wholeness that being in his presence had given her? Would the feeling disappear when he rode away?

Without consciously realizing it, her expression fell and her head tipped toward the ground. Thomas gently lifted her chin with one finger, raising her face until her eyes met his. "I wish I could stay here longer, but I promised I'd be back tonight. I'll come visit you again the first chance I get."

Dicey felt so comfortable with him that without thinking, she threw her arms around his waist and nestled her head in his chest as he encircled her in his arms and pressed his lips to the top of her head. Thomas smiled contentedly as he pulled her back to look into her eyes once more and took her by the hand and led her back to the house.

The birthday party had wound down and the musicians were packing up their instruments as Dicey and Thomas entered the back door. Many of the guests had already departed, but Liz and Samuel sat chatting next to each other in a pair of chairs. Liz lifted her eyes to see her friend enter with the man who had stolen her heart. Liz could tell by the glow on Dicey's face that this one day had changed her friend forever. Liz smiled, observing as Dicey escorted Thomas to the front door where he retrieved his hat, and the pair walked to his horse tied outside.

Thomas fumbled with his hat, "I – I wish we had more time, Dicey."

She reached up and put her arms on his shoulders, pulling him toward her as she kissed the scar on his cheek, "Be careful Thomas," she whispered as concern spread across her brow.

"Don't worry about me, Dicey. I'm as tough as nails," he chuckled. Then tipping his head, he kissed her one last time, lingering only briefly on her soft lips. He replaced his hat, mounted his horse and rode away. Thomas forced himself to ride on without turning back. He felt as if he was leaving a part of himself behind and if he dared to look back, he might lose the courage to go.

Chapter 7

The Coroner met the group of well-respected men outside the front door of the little country schoolhouse.

"Before you go in, I must warn you that this is quite a ghastly sight. Your task in this inquisition is to determine the cause and the perpetrator of what has occurred here."

The group of jurors shook their heads in agreement. As the Coroner opened the door and the line of jurors stepped into the little schoolhouse in Granville County, North Carolina, the stench of death filled Solomon Langston's nostrils.

There hanging from the rafters with a noose about his throat was the town schoolmaster, his neck broken and his body hanging limp and lifeless. Sickened by the sight, Solomon's eyes quickly sought out the floor.

"It is the charge of you good and lawful men to determine by what manner this man's death came and whether he is guilty of taking his own life." The Coroner turned to inspect the body.

The men examined the scene and determined that the schoolmaster had evidently stood on his desk to affix the noose and then stepped off it to kill himself.

MARNIE L. PEHRSON

"Why would he do such a thing – a man with four small children depending upon him?" Christopher Harris, a tall lanky man, shook his head with a combination of disbelief and disgust. "And he'd just purchased over 170 acres of land last year! Makes no sense at all."

"Didn't his wife just die a few months ago?" John White observed.

"He's had a rough time of it since," Robert Allison commented. "I think the grief and the immense responsibility of raising four children by himself was more than he could take."

"Even still! A man has a responsibility to his children!" Solomon exclaimed. "This was a coward's choice it was."

"His mind must not have been right," William Parham suggested.

"Insane or cowardly – neither flatter the man," Solomon reached up to assist the Coroner in lowering the body.

"Then do we have a verdict men?" the Coroner inquired as he, Solomon and Robert Allison laid the body down on a stretcher.

Each man in turn proclaimed his vote and in the end the decision of the inquisition was unanimous – Thomas Springfield was guilty of taking his own life, leaving as orphans his six-year-old daughter Elizabeth and his three sons: Aaron who was nearly eight, Moses who was four, and his namesake little Thomas who had just turned two.

The jury decided that the schoolmaster's belongings should be sold and the proceeds used to care for the children who would soon find themselves divided up into various homes to become apprentices for craftsmen who would care for them until they reached adulthood.

Solomon abruptly sat up in his bed, awakened from the dream that wasn't so much a dream as it was a memory from over a decade ago when he and Sarah lived in Granville County, North Carolina.

"No wonder Thomas Springfield's name rang so familiar! He's the son of that poor deranged schoolmaster who took his own life!" Solomon exclaimed aloud.

Sarah stirred in her bed beside him. "What? Did you say something, dear?" she groggily inquired.

"Yes, Captain Springfield is the son of that schoolmaster who hung himself when we lived in Granville County."

"Pardon?" she rubbed her eyes, still not feeling she was alert enough to understand what he was trying to say.

"Our daughter is involved with the son of a lunatic!" Solomon clad in his nightshirt, held his head in his hands as he rested his elbows on his knees.

"Oh my! But Captain Springfield doesn't appear unstable."

"Neither did his father. Maybe his father was just a coward."

"Captain Springfield is certainly no coward. James assured me of his valiant character. No one could ever accuse him of cowardice!" Sarah defended.

"I suppose not, but still, do you want our daughter marrying into that kind of a family?"

"Surely you don't believe that this type of thing passes from father to son?"

"I don't know. But do we want to risk the possibility?

Sarah Langston stared at her husband in the early light of the morning. "You can't tell Dicey not to see him. She's too headstrong to abide by such a command."

"Then I'll just have to reason with her," Solomon set his feet to the hardwood floor, stood and reached for his trousers, but Sarah Langston knew her daughter well enough to know that Solomon's logic would not sway her in her affections for the Captain.

~*~

Dicey awoke with a glowing smile on her face. Dreams of Thomas lingered sweetly in her mind as she prepared breakfast. Sarah Langston entered the kitchen as Dicey fried bacon at the stove, "Good morning, Mama!" she greeted cheerfully.

"Good morning, Dicey! You look like you had a good night's rest."

"Oh, yes, I did – a wonderful rest," Dicey replied.

Sarah put her arm around her daughter's shoulder, "I like your Captain Springfield. He seems like an amiable fellow, polite and quite handsome."

Dicey beamed, "I'm grateful you approve."

"Did you notice that Beth and James left early yesterday?"

"Yes, I searched for them after Captain Springfield left, but couldn't find them."

"Beth felt sick, so he took her home, but he had to leave again early this morning. I think you need to ride over there today and check on her."

"I'd be happy to," Dicey agreed.

Soon the tromping of footsteps could be heard overhead as Solomon, Henry, Amy, Bennett and Celin descended the stairs for breakfast. The family gathered around the table and after blessing the food the conversation turned to the events of the previous day.

"Mama, Papa - I was so distracted yesterday, I forgot to thank you for the wonderful birthday party you gave me. I loved it!" Dicey's eyes radiated gratitude.

"You're welcome, my dear. I'm glad you enjoyed yourself," her father replied and Sarah shook her head in agreement as she chewed a piece of bacon.

"I think she would have been happy without the party and just the company of Captain Springfield," Henry teased, winking at his sister.

"I saw Dicey kissin' the Captain goodbye," giggled 7-year-old Celin.

Henry feigned a disapproving look, "Dicey! Tsk, tsk, tsk," and started to chuckle.

Dicey's face turned crimson as her eyes issued a stern reprimand and she shook her head indicating that Celin needed to cease her chatter.

Sarah's gaze darted to her husband whose scowl deepened. Sarah, who did not share her husband's concerns about Thomas's chivalry or sanity, changed the subject in an effort to spare Dicey further embarrassment. "I'm sending Dicey to look in on Beth after breakfast. She felt poorly yesterday and James had to leave her to go back to the front."

"Yes, that's a good idea," Solomon agreed, "That poor girl gets awfully lonesome with James gone so much."

Dicey was beginning to understand first hand what Beth must be experiencing and just how much she agonized over James' welfare.

After breakfast, Celin helped Dicey wash the dishes as Henry went outside to feed the livestock. As she walked into the parlor, Dicey was surprised to see her father approaching her with a rifle in his hand.

"Everything all right, Papa?" Dicey's eyebrows furrowed with concern.

"Everything is fine, Dicey. I would just like you to keep this rifle with you. Times are getting more perilous and you need to be prepared for anything. Keep it with you whenever you're out riding."

Dicey wondered what had brought on her father's sudden concern that she should carry a firearm with her at all times and she stared quizzically into his green eyes, "Are you sure everything is all right, Papa?"

"It's fine, Dicey. I just want to make sure that you're safe. After what happened to Samuel Holton Sunday last, I'd just have more peace of mind if I knew you had a rifle handy at all times."

Dicey took the gun from her father, "Thank you, Papa. I'll be careful and keep it with me."

"One more thing, Dicey. Would you please step into my study for a moment?"

"Yes, Sir," she followed him as he limped with his cane and eased into the chair behind his desk.

"I'm not certain how to tell you this, but there's something you need to know about Captain Springfield."

Her eyebrows furrowed. She knew that look on her
father's face all too well. It was the same expression he had
the morning he told her she couldn't deliver messages to her
brothers anymore and when he insisted that she spend less
time riding about the countryside. She felt that sick omen in
the pit of her stomach that her father was about to take away
yet another thing she held dear.

"I knew Captain Springfield's father when we lived in
North Carolina when you were just a toddler."

"You did? Really?" This wasn't what she expected to
hear.

"Yes, he was a kind and gentle man – a schoolmaster – a
talented instructor."

"I would like to have known him. Thomas said his father
and mother passed away when he was a child," Dicey
couldn't help but feel sorry for Thomas for he never had the
comforts of home and the love and nurture of his parents as
she had always experienced.

"Captain Springfield's mother died of an illness and
shortly thereafter the schoolmaster took his own life."

"You mean he…"

"He hanged himself, Dicey," Solomon's stern eyes filled
with an odd foreboding concern. "Right in the middle of the
schoolhouse. I was a jurist in the inquisition."

"How horrible for Thomas!" Dicey exclaimed. "How
painful for him and his brothers and sister!"

"Dicey, I want you to consider something before you
become too involved with Captain Springfield."

Dicey's eyes and nose crinkled with puzzlement.

MARNIE L. PEHRSON

"I want you to consider that Captain Springfield's father was either at worst insane or at the very least a coward, but most likely both. That doesn't bode well for Captain Springfield."

"Papa! Are you trying to suggest that Thomas is somehow a coward or mentally unstable simply because his father took his own life?"

"It's a legitimate possibility that Captain Springfield has inherited his father's instability. There are cases where dementia runs in families. Some people call it 'bad blood.'"

"Papa! You astonish me! Shall we hold the children responsible for the sins of their fathers? What value is our fight for freedom if we do not believe that each individual is free to choose his own path and to make his own way? How free would we be if our destinies were irrevocably chained to the sins of past generations! Captain Springfield is certainly no coward and I refuse to believe that there is anything weak in his mind or character. I do not sense it and I do not believe it!"

Solomon's voice softened, "Dicey, I only meant for you to be careful. Of course he is free to choose his own path, but there are tendencies... tendencies which can run in families."

"May I please be excused now, Sir? I really must be checking on Beth."

Realizing that there was no convincing Dicey when she'd made up her mind, Solomon decided to drop the issue for the moment, "You may be excused, but please ponder upon this a little more, dear."

"There is nothing to ponder, Father. I will not hold Captain Springfield responsible for the sins of his father."

Dicey said nothing further but strode determinedly toward the kitchen and out to the stable where she saddled Gabriel and fastened the rifle in place. She turned to wave goodbye to her mother who stood at the kitchen door, and then mounted her horse and rode in the direction of Beth and James' house.

The entire way she thought about Thomas and the sad life he must have led as an orphan, knowing that his father had taken his own life. How many people had treated him as if he were inferior because of his father's choice? And to think her very own father could be so shallow-minded! She resolutely determined that no one would convince her that Thomas should be considered less of a man because of what his father had done.

When she arrived, no one stirred within the dark house. Dicey led Gabriel to the barn and carried her rifle with her toward the house. She knocked on the front door, but no one came. She jiggled the door handle, but it was locked, so she knocked louder, "Beth, are you in there? It's me, Dicey."

A few moments later, she could hear shuffling footsteps from inside the house, "Dicey is that you?" Beth's voice indicated that she felt pain.

"Yes, Beth, please let me in. Mama sent me to take care of you."

Beth unlatched the door and opened it, "Oh, I'm so relieved to see you, Dicey."

"What's wrong?"

Beth still wore her nightgown, her hair escaped from its braids, and she looked as if she hadn't slept a wink.

"I've got a horrible headache. It's so bad I can't keep my food down."

Dicey turned, bolted the front door and wrapped her arm around her sister-in-law's shoulder and guided her to her bedroom.

"When did James leave?"

"Early this morning. He hated to go, but they were expecting him back."

Tears began to well up in Beth's eyes, "You know, Dicey, in addition to this horrible headache, I have this ominous foreboding that I may never see James again."

Dicey embraced Beth, "Shhh, don't say such things. He'll be fine. You just love him so much that when he leaves it grieves you."

"I do worry, but this time, it feels so much worse." She massaged her temples with her fingertips. "Maybe it's just the headache."

"I'm sure it is" Dicey comforted as she helped Beth into her bed and covered her with blankets. "You get some sleep. I'll go put on some biscuits. Maybe you could keep down a plain biscuit."

"Thank you, Dicey. You're heaven sent," Beth's gratitude caused a fleeting smile to grace her worried brow. Then, she rolled on her side and closed her eyes.

Dicey quietly left the room and shut the door. She entered the kitchen, and began her task. Beth's worries seemed to haunt her as she mixed, rolled and cut the biscuits. A feeling of dread hung within the very walls of the home. Dicey determined that Beth just needed some company to keep her mind off her troubles. As soon as Beth felt up to it, Dicey would take her home with her to stay with their family. Being alone while your husband is away at war would weigh on anyone to an intolerable level.

Dicey pulled the hot biscuits from the oven, placed one on a plate and buttered it lightly. She carried it to Beth's room and gently opened the door. Beth still lay on her side, apparently asleep. Dicey quietly approached her bedside and set the plate on the night table beside her.

Beth's eyes opened, "Thank you, Dicey" she muttered.

"Oh, I'm sorry if I woke you."

"No, you didn't. I've just been lying here with my eyes closed."

"Do you feel up to eating anything?"

"I'll try a morsel," Beth sat up in her bed and Dicey helped her fluff the feather pillows behind her so she could lean back comfortably. Then she handed Beth the buttered biscuit.

Beth took one bite, "Dicey, you make the absolute best biscuits in the world! You simply must teach me your secret."

"I'd be happy to. Matter of fact, I think you should come home with me once you get over this headache. I think staying here alone is just too hard on you. I can teach you then."

Beth shook her head, "Oh no, I couldn't possibly leave. There are the animals to take care of. Who would do that? And what if James came back and I wasn't here?"

"There are ways around all that," Dicey continued.

"I appreciate your concern, Dicey, but I can't leave our home."

"Very well, but if you ever change your mind, our home is always open to you," Dicey let the subject drop. Beth could be a stubborn woman, and there wasn't much point in arguing with her, especially when she felt bad.

"Thank you," Beth smiled, "You know, this biscuit of yours is so delicious that I do believe that it is making me feel a bit better." Beth changed the subject in an effort to lighten the conversation, "I enjoyed meeting your Captain."

A broad grin spread across Dicey's face, "Isn't he handsome?"

"Yes, a very attractive man and he's completely smitten by you," Beth smiled knowingly.

Dicey flushed, "What makes you say that?"

"Besides the fact that he looks at you as if he were a love sick puppy, James told me that you're all the Captain speaks of when they are together. He's asked James to tell him everything about you."

"Really?" Dicey couldn't contain the broad dimpled grin that spread across her face.

"Yes, really."

"So does James see Thomas often?"

"Lately, yes. James is working on a secret mission right now and he reports to Colonel Roebuck at Woods Fort. So he sees the Captain frequently."

"Well, I hope James is selective in what he tells Thomas and doesn't go into all my faults and the foolhardy things I've done in my life."

"I wouldn't count on it. You know what a mischievous, relentless tease James can be."

"You're right about that," Dicey muttered, as she visualized James portraying her as an awkward, laughable, unsophisticated child.

"Thank you for the biscuit, Dicey. My headache is beginning to subside enough now that I think I might be able to sleep," Beth stretched her arms above her head and yawned.

"I will leave you to rest then," Dicey stood, took Beth's plate and moved toward the door. Just as Dicey prepared to leave, Beth added, "Dicey, don't worry about James telling tales on you. There's nothing he could say that could squelch that man's interest in you."

"I hope you're right," Dicey shook her head and left the room, closing it behind her.

She returned to the kitchen and as she washed the dishes, her thoughts turned to all the foolish things she'd done growing up and what stories James could tell on her. She could just see him enlightening Thomas of the time she took the shortcut through the bull pen when she was eight and was nearly gored in the rear.

Then there was the time that James taught her how to ride a horse. She was atop Gabriel right after she got him. Solomon, who loved to pester his sister, smacked the horse on the rump. Gabriel startled, reared up on his hind legs, and threw her up into the air to land smack in the middle of a hot steamy cow patty! James and Solomon still laughed about that whenever they got together. Even Dicey found herself smiling just thinking about it.

She decided she'd get her mind off James' talebearing by reading a book. She entered James' study to find one. James, an avid reader, had a fine collection of books. Dicey pulled a volume of Shakespearian sonnets from the shelf. She nestled into a rocking chair in James' study and flipped through the pages. The book opened to Shakespeare's Sonnet 116:

Let me not to the marriage of true minds
>   Admit impediments. Love is not love
Which alters when it alteration finds,
>   Or bends with the remover to remove:

O no! it is an ever-fixed mark
>   That looks on tempests and is never shaken;
It is the star to every wandering bark,
>   Whose worth's unknown, although his height be taken.

Love's not Time's fool, though rosy lips and cheeks
>   Within his bending sickle's compass come:
Love alters not with his brief hours and weeks,
>   But bears it out even to the edge of doom.

If this be error and upon me proved,
>   I never writ, nor no man ever loved.

Dicey leaned her head back and held the open book to her bosom. Perhaps Thomas' feelings would not alter toward her even if James told his embarrassing stories. Dicey closed her eyes and drifted off to sleep with thoughts of Thomas wafting through her mind.

Suddenly Dicey awoke to a shocking pounding at the front door. A sudden rush of adrenaline coursing through her veins, she leapt to her feet, dropping the book to the floor. She immediately crossed to the foyer of the home and grabbed her father's rifle.

"Open up, James Langston! We know you're in there!" came a gruff demanding voice from the other side of the door as fists pounded even more furiously than before.

Dicey took position in front of the door, breathing heavily as she debated on how to respond. Should she ignore them and pretend no one was home? Should she clatter about as if there were many people inside ready to retaliate? She couldn't take the chance on them busting through the door. She'd allowed one set of cowboys to ransack her family's home, she quickly determined that she wasn't going to allow another group to intrude upon James and Beth's. She held her breath and offered a quick silent prayer for strength. Her voice carried forth calmly yet forcefully, "Who is it and what do you want?"

"Let us in, we know James is there," the knob jiggled and the entire doorframe shook with the force of the pressure on the other side. She aimed the barrel of the rifle at the door.

"James is not here. This is his sister. I've come to take care of his ailing wife. He is not here, and we have no idea when he will be back. You either leave now or I'll be forced to use this rifle on you."

"You think we're scared of a woman?" their pounding increased to a fierce, vehement, house-rattling extreme.

Although her body literally trembled, Dicey's voice remained stern and authoritative, "You ought to be scared of me. I'm an expert marksman. You attempt to enter this door and believe me, I will not hesitate to fill you full of lead."

Her voice became so insistent and determined that the men ceased their pounding and turned to one another puzzled. A large burly man with a day of dark beard growth turned to his companion. "I don't think he's here. James Langston would never hide behind a woman's skirts."

"I think you're right," the second man agreed.

"We'll take you at your word, Miss Langston, but if we discover that you have lied to us and James is here, we'll hunt you down and make you pay a price before we execute you."

"I told you James is not here. You can be on your way," Dicey added determinedly.

Dicey stood by the door listening to the silence and then heard horse hooves as the two men rode away.

She stood in readiness until she felt assured that the men were gone and would not return. She leaned the rifle against the wall by the door and paced the room, *Beth cannot stay here. It's just too dangerous. Heaven help us!* She began to pray and plead for the safety of her family and especially James.

Dicey stood guard for several hours before she heard Beth stirring inside her room. Dicey tapped gently on the door, "Beth, may I come in?"

"Yes, Dicey," she answered.

As Dicey entered the room, she noted that Beth had dressed herself, fixed her hair and appeared infinitely better than the disheveled state in which Dicey had originally found her. "Beth, did you sleep through the whole thing?"

"What whole thing?"

"Two men came to the door and nearly pounded it down trying to get in. I held them off with Papa's rifle and they left a few hours ago."

Beth's face expressed alarm, "Really? I didn't hear anything. I slept so soundly." Beth began touching Dicey's face and arms examining her for cuts, bruises or evidence of violence, "Are you all right?"

"I'm fine. They didn't get in. But they were looking for James. You *must* leave here. I've figured it all out. You'll ride with me to our house and I'll send Papa and Henry to get your livestock. But you can't stay here. It's just too dangerous."

Dicey insisted so determinedly that Beth didn't even quibble. She acknowledged the unyielding determination in Dicey's eyes and knew there would be no swaying her, "I'll pack a bag of clothes." She hurried to her dresser and frantically pulled bloomers, petticoats and corsets from the drawers.

"Take anything of value with you. There's a high probability that they will return and ransack the house," Dicey added.

Beth's head popped up from rummaging through the drawer, "You really think so?"

"Nothing's safe. I'll go through the house and gather anything that would interest them."

As Dicey turned toward the door, Beth called after her, "But what about James? What if he comes while I'm gone? He'll be frightfully worried."

"We'll leave him a note so he'll know where you are and put it somewhere he'll see. I'll go downstairs and write it now."

As Beth gathered her belongings, Dicey went to James' study and noted the book of Shakespearian sonnets that lay on the ground beside the rocking chair. She gently lifted it, straightened the pages and set it on the desk. She pulled some parchment from the desk drawer and dipped the quill in ink and began her note.

James, I have taken Beth with me to our house. She misses you terribly and it's not safe here. Come for her there. Be careful, my dear brother. With Love – Dicey

Dicey picked up the volume of sonnets, carried them to the kitchen, laid the note on the kitchen table and placed a cup on the edge of the paper to weight it down. She then began gathering items of value from the house and placing them in a sack. She decided she'd borrow the sonnets and added the volume to the sack. Beth came from her bedroom carrying a bag in which she had placed her clothing

"I'm going to borrow one of James' books. Is that all right?"

"My goodness, Dicey, borrow anything you'd like. You don't need to ask."

Dicey smiled at her sister-in-law, "Examine what I've gathered here and see if there's anything else you think we should take, and we'll be on our way."

Beth added to the sack a family Bible, a small framed portrait which she had painted of James, and a handcrafted jewelry box which James made for her as a gift for their first wedding anniversary. The ladies quickly left through the back door and briskly approached the barn. Dicey saddled Beth's horse, and fastened her bags to the animal. She helped Beth climb onto the horse, and then mounted Gabriel, holding her rifle in her arms as she rode.

"Let's go," Dicey led out and Beth followed. Beth took one last wistful look back toward her home and then caught up to Dicey, riding alongside her. While Beth was an adequate rider, Dicey didn't travel as fast as she normally would so that the journey would be easier for Beth.

They arrived without event at the Langston plantation and the ladies took their horses around to the barn, removed their saddles and carried their bags toward the house. Sarah Langston emerged from the kitchen and met them half way, extending her hand to take a bag, "What are you girls doing here with all these belongings?" An expression of concern infused her elegant face.

"Mama, two men tried to break in on us. They were looking for James. I sent them away and told them he wasn't there. We waited a few hours until everything was safe and I decided it would be best if Beth came to stay with us," Dicey explained.

"Oh my!" Sarah threw her hand to her mouth. "Yes, you acted wisely, Dicey." Sarah could see the tears welling up in Beth's eyes. She put her arm around her daughter-in-law and guided her to the house. "Don't worry dear, everything will be all right."

They entered the house. "You can sleep in James and Solomon's old room," Sarah explained as she carried Beth's personal belongings in her hand and guided her upstairs.

Dicey followed carrying a bag of valuables. "Beth, you settle in here and get some rest. Dicey and I'll go make dinner and call you when it's ready."

~*~

Beth stayed with the Langstons until June arrived. She seemed to brighten and become more hopeful under their protective care and encouraging company. She joined Dicey and Sarah as they cooked, sewed and cleaned.

While her days were spent in pleasant surroundings, she would still awake often in the middle of the night with a nightmare about James. Sometimes she'd call out to him and Dicey would come running from the next room to comfort her.

Moisture hung thickly in the mid-June morning air. While the sun had not yet reached its full apex overhead, the heat of the day was soon upon her as Dicey picked fruit from a cluster of blueberry bushes in the front yard. The June bugs swarmed around her and she swatted the annoying insects from her face with her handkerchief and then captured the perspiration from her forehead with the lacy cloth. She shoved the handkerchief into the bosom of her dress and reached up to pull down a heavily laden limb of sweet berries. Henry and Celin were supposed to be helping her, but they ate more than what accumulated into their buckets.

132

"You two aren't fit for nothin'" she chided. "You may as well just stop picking if you're going to eat more than you gather. I'm trying to make a cobbler, you know."

Taking her suggestion, Henry pulled a string from his pocket and caught a June bug in his fist. He picked it up in his other hand, holding it between his thumb and forefinger. "It's so ugly!" Celin gasped, "How can you stand to touch it?"

"Here I'll hold it still, and you tie the string around its leg, Celin," Henry instructed.

Celin tied the string to the insect's leg and then she squealed with delight as Henry released it and the June bug took flight on the other end of the string. She held the string tightly in her little hands as the bug swarmed around seeking its freedom.

The three of them turned toward the road when they heard the fast beating of horse hooves. Upon recognizing who approached, Dicey set down her bucket of berries, lifted her skirts and they scurried enthusiastically toward the house, Celin dragging the poor June bug behind her as she ran.

"Solomon!" Dicey and Henry called out in unison. Their twenty-one-year-old brother, Solomon, handsome in his military uniform, had their mother's dark brown hair and eyes, but stood shorter and stockier than James or Henry. Solomon had returned to the military after a short leave in the spring to be with his wife and new baby, and so it had been several months since the family had seen him.

Solomon turned to wave at them as they approached. He dismounted his horse and barely had time to tie it at the front of the house before Dicey, Henry and Celin mobbed him, throwing their arms around him and Dicey planted a kiss firmly on his cheek, "We haven't seen you in so long, Solomon! How are you?" Dicey pulled back to examine his face.

"I – I'm just fine, Dicey, thank you," he answered hesitantly.

Dicey knew something must be wrong by the expression on his face. "Solomon, what is it?"

"I have some news, but I'd prefer to tell the whole family at once."

Dicey felt a sick sinking feeling in the pit of her stomach. Something felt terribly wrong.

As the four entered the front door of the residence, they were met by their parents and Beth. Little Amy tugged on her mother's dress as Bennett came running from the kitchen. Sarah and Solomon hurried to their son, each embracing him. "Sol, my boy! What a joy it is to have you home!" his father greeted as Sarah kissed his cheek and hugged him ardently.

She too observed the sorrow which began to well up as tears in his eyes.

Sarah covered her mouth with her hands, "Solomon, something's wrong. What is it?"

Solomon fidgeted with his hat in his hands, looking toward the floor. "I don't know how to tell you all this." He wiped at the inside corners of his eyes with his thumb and forefinger.

His father put his arm around him, "Tell us, son. What is it?"

"It's James, he uh –"

Beth sank to the floor and began to weep, "I knew it. I knew something was terribly wrong," she muttered through her tears.

"What's happened to James?" Dicey grabbed her brother's arm as Sarah knelt down next to Beth and wrapped her arms around her daughter-in-law, allowing her to cry on her shoulder.

"The Tories have been after him for months. The Farrows hemmed him into a house the other night. He put up quite a fight and killed several of them in his effort to escape, but he – he didn't make it. The men from Woods fort found his body last night."

"No, James, No!" Beth cried out.

"Are you sure? Are they absolutely certain it's James?" his father questioned as he grasped his son's arm.

"Yes, they're sure. They sent for me and I confirmed it this morning before I rode here to tell you."

Dicey felt numb. How could this be? How could James be dead? He always seemed so invincible. She could see his kind eyes smiling down at her. She thought of the morning she'd crossed the river and how he'd snuck up and scared her while she gathered eggs. She remembered her twelfth birthday when James surprised her with Gabriel and spent weeks teaching her how to ride. She could see his eyebrows raise and lower mischievously when Thomas walked in behind him on her birthday.

Dicey stumbled backward and plopped into a chair, burying her head in her hands as the tears streaming down her face turned into heartbroken sobs. She grew so distraught that she didn't notice the pain and tears of her family members as they tried to console one another.

Knowing how close Dicey and James were, her brother Solomon gave her a few moments and then squatted down in front of her. He put a hand gently on her shoulder, "Dicey."

She looked up at him momentarily through her tears and then threw her arms around his neck, "Oh Solomon! Not James! Not James!" she sobbed.

Solomon's tears commingled with hers as they held each other. No one spoke for nearly half an hour and finally Sarah broke the silence, "What about his body, Solomon? Will they bring him to us?"

"Colonel Roebuck told me to run ahead and tell you and that he would send some men later this afternoon with James' body."

With the mention of James' body, Beth could take nothing more. She sprang from the floor and darted up the stairs and into her room – James' room. She flung herself onto the bed feeling as if her heart had split in two.

"Poor Beth!" Dicey exclaimed as she rose and trailed her sister-in-law.

Sarah grabbed Dicey by the shoulders, "Leave her be for now, Dicey. She needs some time to grieve."

"She shouldn't be alone," Dicey objected and she forced her way past her mother and darted up the stairs. She approached the door to Beth's room, wondering what in the world she could possibly say to comfort her. She placed her small hand on the door and mustered the courage to speak, "Beth, may I come in?"

She heard only heartbroken sobs from inside the room, Dicey tried the knob, but it was locked. She waited a moment, and decided that perhaps her mother was right and that Beth just wanted some time to herself. As Dicey turned to leave, Beth's door opened and she walked into the hallway and flung her arms around Dicey's neck, weeping bitter tears. Dicey didn't say anything. There were no words that could make a difference so she held her and cried along with her.

Finally Beth broke from her embrace, brushing her tear stained cheeks with the palms of her hands. "Thank you, Dicey, for being here for me. I know you're dying inside too. I just need to be alone now." She turned and went back to her room and shut the door.

Dicey debated upon whether to go to her own room, but decided she couldn't stand the horrible feeling that hung in the air. She needed to breathe in the sunshine, not the stale fog of grief that filled their home. She descended the stairs, went out the back door, and ran to her favorite place – the bench under the weeping willow overlooking the pond.

Had it really been only last month that she sat here with Thomas on her birthday? The happiness and carefree atmosphere of that day seemed like a lifetime ago. Would she ever know happiness again? She thought not. Dicey stared at the pond in utter disbelief for perhaps an hour, when suddenly she had the distinct feeling that someone watched her.

She turned her head back toward the house, and to her complete astonishment, Thomas in his military uniform stood gazing at her, an expression of profound sorrow in his blue eyes. Not trusting her vision, she rubbed her eyes with her handkerchief and shook her head in disbelief.

"I heard the news, Dicey. I'm so incredibly sorry," he took a step toward her and she rose from her seat and ran to him. Throwing her arms around his waist, she leaned her head on his broad chest. He kissed the top of her head and encircled her in his arms.

In the comfort of Thomas' embrace, there sparked a glimmer of hope that perhaps one day she might find happiness again, but then she thought of poor Beth. Beth would never again feel her husband's arms around her. How could she survive without the man she loved? Tears began to flow once more, covering Thomas' shirt, soaking his chest as her heart broke for her sister-in-law.

Dicey dabbed at his muscular chest with her handkerchief, "I'm so sorry, I've soaked your shirt," she apologized.

Thomas took her face in his hands, "Don't worry about it Dicey. That's why I'm here."

At that moment, she realized what she must look like all swollen-eyed and runny-nosed. She shook her head, "I must look a fright," she began as she dabbed at her face with her handkerchief.

"You look beautiful."

"Oh, yes, I'm sure I do!" she quipped sarcastically as she turned from him and started briskly toward the pond, drying her tears and blowing her nose as she went.

He caught up to her and put his arm around her shoulder, and she leaned her head on his side and slipped her arm around his waist.

"I need a long walk to clear my head," she stated in an effort to regain her composure.

Then the realization struck her, "So if you're here, does that mean you came with the men from Woods Fort who brought his – the body?"

"Yes" he whispered.

Dicey looked instinctively back to the house, but Thomas redirected her attention, pulling her onward, "Don't think about that now, Dicey, let's walk in the orchards."

Dicey breathed deeply, snubbing occasionally from the tears that refused to let her forget that her heart broke with pain. Her head felt as if it were being crushed in a vice.

After meandering for some time in the orchard, Dicey released herself from Thomas' arm and leaned her hand against a particularly large apple tree, "In the fall, this tree has the sweetest apples in the whole orchard. When I was little, James used to climb to the top and bring each of us down a huge, juicy apple." She leaned her back against the tree and let her head rest on the trunk, closing her eyes as if remembering a fond memory from her childhood. "He'd fill a big bucket with water and we'd bob for apples. Sol would always try to distract me by pulling my pigtails when it was my turn, and James would hold him back so that I had a fair chance. James always looked out for me."

"And you looked out for him, too, didn't you?" Thomas added.

"Not this time," she thought to herself and looked away from him.

Thomas stepped closer and stood facing her, reaching up to stretch his left arm, and grasping a high limb above her head with his hand. He lovingly brushed away her tears with this right. "You know you'll see him again don't you, Dicey? We're just travelers here. You'll be with your brother again one day in a much sweeter place than even these apple orchards."

Dicey opened her eyes to look up into his and at that moment she knew it. She knew she loved this man who had come to console her in her darkest hour. She also knew in her soul that he spoke the truth. Death would not be the end and one day she would see her precious James again. She smiled through her tears, "Thank you Thomas, for reminding me of that. Thank you for being here to comfort me."

He reached forward and brushed the fresh tears from each of her cheeks, and cradled her face in his hands. He knew intimately the loneliness, fear and pain that accompanied the loss of a loved one. Even though he was only two when his parents died, every day of his life he mourned their loss and the only thing that brought him peace was hoping that he would be with his parents again on some heavenly shore. Many had told him that it would more likely be hell's gates at which he would greet his father, but Thomas refused to believe that there could not be some hope for his heartbroken parent. He'd spent many sleepless nights pondering on what would make a man become so desperate with loss that he would take his own life.

He never could understand it until this moment that he came to realize the intensity of his feelings for the woman who stood before him. Could he bear it if she were torn from his life as his mother had been ripped from his father's?

140

"I had to come. I..." Thomas hesitated as she stared up at him with those striking chocolate brown eyes. His own glistened with moisture, for he could not bear to see her in such pain, "I couldn't allow you to be alone today. I – I love you, Dicey."

Dicey swallowed hard. Did he really just say what she thought he said? He tipped his head down and gently kissed her cheeks and then her lips. "I love you too, Thomas," she whispered as she put her hands around his neck and they lost themselves in each other's embrace.

Finally she pulled herself back. "I've cried so much that I'm exhausted," she announced as she leaned her head back against the tree and Thomas' hand slid from her cheek to her neck, caressing her soft skin with his thumb.

"Here ..." He took her by the shoulders, pulling her toward him and then positioned himself behind her so that his back leaned against the tree. "Let's sit for a while. He sat down, leaned against the tree and tugged her hand indicating that she should sit in front of him. She sat down and he pulled her to rest her back comfortably against his chest.

Thomas encircled her waist with his arms, "There, now just lean back against me and rest a while." Dicey breathed deeply, drinking in the smell of him – that comforting aroma of wool and a roaring fire. Soon she drifted off to sleep in Thomas' arms.

"Don't ever leave me, Thomas," she muttered.

Thomas wasn't sure if she was awake or asleep. He leaned forward and kissed her rosy cheek, "I'm here Dicey. I'm not going anywhere."

How could he leave her now, he wondered? He resolved to stay with her at least through the funeral. He didn't care if they court marshaled him for desertion. He wouldn't leave her now.

~*~

Thomas obtained leave from the military to stay with the Langstons until the day after James' funeral. Family and friends came from miles around to pay their respects to the lovable and kindhearted Patriot. They held the funeral in the Langston home and Solomon and Sarah spared no expense in providing a lavish assortment of food and beverages for those who attended. Thomas continued to be a constant comfort to Dicey and over the next few days they grew closer.

With the subject of death thick in the air, Thomas confided in her the story of his father who had hanged himself after his wife Martha's passing. His father who held a solid position as schoolmaster and owned over 170 acres in land could have easily found another wife to help him raise his children, but he was too heartbroken and unstable to imagine life without her.

For years Thomas had been angry with his father, unable to comprehend the cowardice of a man who would give up on life and leave his four little children to fend for themselves. Thomas determined to devote himself to duty, honor and responsibility. It was his sense of duty and honor which propelled him onward courageously in the Patriot cause.

Now, as a grown man, in love for the first time, he could better understand his father's unstable behavior. Thomas knew himself well enough to feel confident that he would never relinquish his duty to those who depended upon him, but he could better understand the feelings his father must have experienced. Thomas need only imagine for an instant that something could happen to Dicey and the emotions of pain, loss and loneliness thickened within the walls of his chest. For a fleeting moment, he could conceive that death would be preferable.

~*~

The morning after the funeral, Dicey rose early as usual to prepare breakfast. Thomas lay awake in his bed in Henry's room, fully dressed, waiting for Dicey to emerge from her room. When he heard her door creek open and her light footsteps descending the stairs, he waited a minute and then quietly crept down the stairs and snuck up behind her were she stood preparing donuts. He threw his arms around her waist, lifted her slightly off the ground, and kissed her neck.

Dicey, smacked at his arms that surrounded her small waist, "Thomas, you scared me!" As he set her feet back on the floor, she spun around to face his broad chuckling grin and twinkling blue eyes.

"Good mornin'!" he greeted jovially and gave her a peck on the lips.

"I've got flour all over my hands, Thomas. I'm going to soil your uniform and the Colonel won't be too pleased about that," she scolded holding her hands up in the air in front of her face and wiggling to free herself from his arms.

"I think it would be worth it," he teased.

"Well if you don't mind getting flour-dusted, then help me with these donuts," she reached down and wiped her hands on her apron, and then grabbed another apron from the back of a chair and handed it to him.

"Here, put this on and help me." Dicey tried to sound scolding, but she couldn't keep the smile from creeping back over her lips.

Thomas took the apron and tied it about his waist. "All right, teach me how you make these delicious donuts." He inhaled deeply, enjoying the smell of the sweet dough.

"Well, the dough has already been rising overnight, so we just need to cut and fry them now," she instructed as she rolled out the dough with a rolling pin and handed Thomas the cutter. "Dip it in the flour so it doesn't stick to the dough."

Thomas helped Dicey, but occasionally stole the donut holes and popped them into his mouth when her attention was turned. She glanced up to see him chewing a mouthful of dough, "Thomas Springfield! You're as bad as little Bennett! Stop eating all the dough or we won't have any donuts."

He looked like a child with his hand caught in the cookie jar, "Sorry" he mumbled with his mouth full of sticky dough. He struggled to quickly swallow the dough then added, "You know I'm going to eat more than anyone else anyway. What does it matter if I eat them raw or cooked?" he grinned mischievously.

Dicey rolled her eyes, took a blob of dough she held in her hand and swiped it on the bridge of his nose.

He reached up, pinched the dough from his face and ate it, "Thank you!" he grinned.

About that time, Sarah Langston entered the kitchen, "You two having fun this morning?"

"Yes Ma'am!" Thomas answered enthusiastically.

"We're going to miss you, Captain Springfield. You already feel like one of the family," Sarah patted his shoulder as she passed him on her way to the stove. Sarah Langston had no idea just how much her words meant to him.

The smile fled from Dicey's face at the reminder that Thomas would be leaving today, and she worked more furiously rolling out the dough in front of her.

"I'll get the oil heating for you," Sarah offered as she placed a large iron pot on the stove.

Thomas noticed Dicey's change in demeanor, and leaned over to kiss her cheek. Her smile immediately returned, but then she pointed her eyes toward her mother's back and shook her head sternly indicating that he needed to be less affectionate while her mother remained in the room.

Thomas glanced at her mother's back, shrugged his shoulders and kissed Dicey full on the lips. At just that moment, Sarah Langston turned around to grab a towel from the table.

"Dicey Langston!" she exclaimed as she found her daughter returning the young Captain's kiss, "I'm right here in the room you know!"

Dicey pulled back quickly, her face now crimson. She threw a donut center at Thomas. "See there, you got me in trouble!" she fussed.

The dough bounced off his chest, and he caught it in his hand and tossed it into his mouth.

"Ain't nothin' sweeter," he winked at Dicey as he cleaned his hands on his apron, untied it from his waist, and laid it on the back of a chair. Then he leaned over to whisper in her ear, "And I ain't talkin' about the donut."

Thomas walked toward the door, "I better go prepare my horse to leave."

That's a fine thing to do to me, Thomas Springfield! Leave me alone with Mama after you get me in trouble, she scolded him in her thoughts as she avoided her mother's gaze. Several minutes of silence passed between them.

"So do you have something to tell me?" Sarah coaxed.

"What do you mean?" Dicey kept working with the dough in front of her.

"About you and the Captain? Is there anything you want to tell me?"

"What's to tell? I don't know what you mean, Mama?" Dicey' puzzled expression wrinkled her brow.

"Do I hear wedding bells?" her mother smiled.

"No, no wedding bells," Dicey shook her head, "Are you trying to get rid of me, Mama?"

"Why no, dear! I'd love to have you right here with me always, but only a fool could miss that you two are well on your way to the altar."

"Well, not yet," Dicey felt the hot blush of embarrassment at her mother's question, but it did give her cause to ponder.

Sarah's voice lowered to a whisper, "Your Papa told me about the Captain's father. Has Captain Springfield spoken with you about it yet?"

Dicey took a more determined stance as if she were about to shoulder a weapon and brace for impact, "Yes, we discussed it. It weighs heavily on his mind, but I assure you, Mama, that there is nothing unstable about Captain Springfield." Dicey shook her head determinedly.

"I know dear. Your father just worries about you," a smile crossed Sarah's eyes letting her know that she would be her advocate on the matter.

"There's really nothing to worry about. Will you talk with Papa for me and assure him of that?"

"I will speak with him," Sarah nodded and turned back toward the stove.

~*~

After breakfast, Thomas helped Dicey wash dishes. "I've got to leave after we finish these," he mumbled.

"Then, let's dirty some more," she teased, attempting to make light of the moment in order to keep the tears from welling up in her eyes.

"I don't think the Colonel would take an unending pile of dishes as an excuse," he chuckled.

Thomas finished drying the last dish and put it in the cupboard, "Well, I guess that is that." He began brushing a wet spot on his shirt with the towel. "I'll bid your parents farewell."

"I'll meet you outside," she said as she turned and went out the kitchen door and toward the stables. Her heart started to ache and the lump that had formed in her throat burned with intensity from her attempt to hold her emotions at bay. She hated this feeling. Her nerves were so raw over the last few days that Thomas had seen her cry more than any man should have to endure a woman's tears. She angrily brushed the moisture from her eyes.

Thomas sauntered out of the kitchen carrying his bag over his shoulder and his rifle in his hand. In silence, he flung the bag onto the back of his horse and secured it along with his rifle to the saddle. He turned to face her. Thomas swallowed, trying to remove the lump that had settled in his throat.

"I hate this," he muttered.

"Me too," she hesitated and then questioned, "What do you hate?"

"Leaving you," he replied.

Dicey could feel the tears stinging her eyes, "Please be careful, Thomas," she threw her hands around his neck, kissed his cheek and turned to run toward the house. She didn't want the vision of her that he carried with him to be one of her tear-stained face. He'd seen enough of her that way.

Thomas caught Dicey by the arm and pulled her back toward him, encircling her in his arms, "Where are you going?"

Dicey buried her face in his chest, breathing in the scent of him, and threw her arms around him as tears rolled down her cheeks, "Promise me you'll be careful, Thomas."

"Nothing's going to happen to me, Dicey," he lifted her chin with his finger so that she would look up at him.

"I just couldn't take it..." she dared not finish the sentence. *"I just couldn't take losing you too. As much as it's devastated me to lose James, I would never recover if I lost you."*

"Dicey, listen to me. The war is winding to a close. We've made great progress in driving the British out of South

Carolina. It will all be over soon and when it is, we don't ever have to be apart again."

"But all of that didn't help James," tears began to flow from her eyes.

"I'm not James, Dicey. James was a hero. The Tories hated him. They killed him for revenge. They don't even know or care that I exist. I'm just an ordinary soldier."

"You are no ordinary soldier, Thomas."

"You know what I mean. I'll be fine. Trust me."

She forced a smile and dabbed the tears from her eyes with her handkerchief.

"Now give me a kiss to carry with me," his eyes twinkled teasingly.

Dicey bit her lip to stifle the embarrassing smile that threatened her dimpled cheeks. And then he washed away all her tears and her fears with one last loving embrace that would need to last them both until they met again.

Chapter 8

On a hot late-June afternoon beads of perspiration ran down Dicey's temples as she stood on a stool picking blueberries. She reached up on her tip toes to pull down a heavy laden limb and raked the blueberries into the bucket that hung on her forearm.

"Dicey, I have wonderful news!" Liz hurried to where Dicey worked.

"Liz! Hello! It's so grand to see you!" Dicey stepped down from the footstool and approached her friend, "What's your news?"

"Samuel bought a small piece of property on the other side of town using the money he's saved and he's starting on a cabin next week."

"Really? That sounds exciting."

"He's asked me to marry him!" Liz hugged Dicey enthusiastically.

"That's the best news I've heard in months!" Dicey embraced Liz excitedly, "So when is the wedding?"

"We haven't set a date yet, but it will be as soon as he can get the cabin built and afford to buy some livestock to start farming. Probably in the spring."

"I'm so happy for you, Liz!"

"Mother and Father are excited about it too. Of course, Father doesn't know about Samuel's family's financial problems. But we have informed him that Samuel and I want to stand on our own two feet."

"What does he think of that?" Dicey asked.

"He seems impressed that Samuel's willing to work hard and make his own way."

"I'm so glad you two are not letting his father's financial problems stand in your way!" Dicey felt proud of her friend for cherishing the important things in life and not being bound to her fine possessions so much that she would let them keep her from marrying a good man who loved her.

"So what ever happened with Matthew Love? Is Samuel still associating with him?" Dicey hadn't had time alone with Liz since before the funeral, so she wondered what had become of the relationship between Samuel and the Bloody Scout.

"Not since Mr. Love left our house. As you know, he only stayed a few days and then his family took him home. Samuel hasn't seen him since, and I've asked him not to. I think he realizes now how dangerous that association can be," Liz explained.

"I'd say so. Mr. Holton is fortunate that he's alive!" Dicey's anxiety grew evident.

"I know! Thank you again for helping us through that whole ordeal. I don't know what I would have done without you there!" gratitude surfaced in Liz's pale blue eyes as she shook her head remembering that traumatic day.

"So how have you and your family been? How is poor Beth?" Liz's brow furrowed with anxiety.

"Beth is getting by. Her parents came to take her home to Spartanburg with them earlier this week. I'm missing her terribly. But I know it's best for her to put some distance between herself and all the memories. She needs time to heal, and being here with us held too many reminders of James."

"That makes sense. Poor woman! How about your parents?"

"Mama and Papa are holding up tolerably well. Of course, Mama will tear up every now and then and I know she cries a lot when the rest of us aren't around. I'm having a hard enough time myself, I don't know how I could bear what Mama or Beth are going through right now," Dicey shook her head, feeling the pain of her mother and Beth.

"I'm just so sorry for all of you," Liz put a comforting arm about her friend, "Here, let me help you pick berries. I'm tall. I can reach the higher limbs for you."

Dicey and Liz picked blueberries together in silence for a few minutes, eating an occasional sweet berry. Liz turned to Dicey and smiled, "I'm so happy that you and Captain Springfield were able to spend a few days together!"

"Oh, I don't know how I could have made it through without him, Liz. He's such a comfort to me." Emotion broke through in Dicey's voice. "I didn't want to let him go."

"You love him, don't you Dicey," Liz stated matter-of-factly.

"Yes, I do. It's hard to explain how someone you haven't known that long feels like someone you've known forever."

"I know exactly what you mean," Liz smiled.

"Yes, I suppose you do, don't you!" Dicey's dimpled grin spread across her face as she looked at her friend and thought how blessed they were to have each other to share these experiences together.

Dicey glanced down at her bucket of blueberries as Liz put another handful in, "I think we have enough for three pies, Liz. We can stop now."

"I'd enjoy helping you make them," Liz offered enthusiastically.

"Thank you, I'd love to spend some more time with you," Dicey felt grateful for the company. The loneliness of losing James, Beth leaving and Thomas' departure had started to wear on her.

The two girls carried their berries toward the house. Bennett and Amy played on the front porch with a small wagon that James had made for them a few years prior. Streams of perspiration rolled down from Bennett's tousled brown hair, leaving streaks on his dirty little face. He'd worked up quite a sweat tugging Amy along in the wagon after they'd spent the morning making mud pies.

"You're going to need a good bath tonight, Bennett! You're a mess!" Dicey chided as she rubbed her hand on the top of his head, mussing his hair as she passed him. "Don't wear yourself out," she called back as she entered the house and Liz followed her.

"They are just so cute!" Liz looked back over her shoulder and smiled at the children.

Liz followed Dicey to the kitchen and the two young women began preparing the blueberry pies. Dicey enjoyed Liz's lighthearted company and listened to her talk about her

153

wedding plans, the dress her mother was making for her, and her ideas for beautifying her new home.

As Dicey placed the pies in the oven, she heard horses approach the house. Dicey peeked her head out of the kitchen to see who her father greeted at the door. He invited three men into the home, talking with them briefly at the front door.

"Who are they?" Liz inquired.

"Whigs," Dicey answered, "I suppose they've come to pay their respects to Papa."

"Oh" Liz took a wash cloth and began wiping down the flour-dusted table and placing the utensils in the dishpan.

Dicey continued to keep an eye on the men as her father led them into his study and shut the door. She recognized Paul Webb, a prematurely gray-haired man. James had associated with the likeable and fun-loving Mr. Webb quite frequently. He had always been kind to Dicey and she was happy to see him again.

Another sandy-haired man of stocky build whom she'd seen before accompanied Mr. Webb. She didn't know his name, but she did know William Frederick, a tall, wiry, red-haired hot-head that made James uneasy. Dicey remembered James commenting that Frederick acted more like a Bloody Scout than a Patriot. His methods were barbaric and he'd been accused of raping a Tory's wife after looting her home while her husband fought in the war. Dicey felt uneasy with him in their home and hoped that her father would get rid of him as quickly as possible.

Dicey and Liz sat down at the kitchen table across from each other, "So how does it feel to be engaged?" Dicey leaned her head on her hands and stared at Liz, anxiously awaiting her reply.

"Wonderful!" Liz fidgeted nervously, her long slender fingers twirling and interlacing her apron ties. "And a little frightening too," she added.

"Frightening?" Dicey raised her eyebrows in surprise at Liz's choice of words.

"Well, maybe I should say nervous. But it is kind of frightening if you think about it – being on your own, being married, starting a family and a home from scratch."

"Oh, I see what you mean," Dicey nodded.

Dicey gazed out the window and pondered on what it would be like to start a home and raise a family with Thomas. Would she find it frightening she wondered? Exciting, adventurous, and absolutely wonderful – yes, but frightening would not be a word she would have chosen. No, she felt so perfectly comfortable and at peace with Thomas that she could never feel frightened when he stood near. Her mind darted back to the afternoon that she fell asleep in his arms at the base of the apple tree.

"What are you thinking about, Dicey?" Liz noticed the faraway look in her friend's eyes.

Startled back to the present, Dicey turned toward Liz, "Just thinking about what it would feel like to be getting married and starting your own home and family. I'm envious!" she smiled.

"Oh, you and Captain Springfield will be getting married before you know it," Liz encouraged. "Has he mentioned anything about marriage to you?"

"No, not yet. But he did tell me he loved me," she beamed. "And he said that the war would be over soon and then we'd never have to be apart again. So I think he's thought about it."

"Oh Dicey! That's wonderful! I hope you two live close to us so we can raise our children together!"

"Wouldn't that be marvelous!" Dicey agreed excitedly.

~*~

Dicey pulled the hot pies out of the oven just as her father and the three men came out of Solomon's study and into the parlor. "Would you lads like a slice of pie?" Solomon offered as he limped with his cane toward the kitchen.

"Thank you, yes," replied Mr. Frederick, a slimy smile spreading across his pale freckled face.

Agitation welled in Dicey that her father would ask them to stay. She didn't mind sharing the pie – especially not with Mr. Webb or the other man, but Mr. Frederick gave her a sickening feeling in the pit of her stomach. The sooner he left their home the better.

Sarah Langston entered the kitchen and the three men followed. Dicey smiled at Mr. Webb as he took her hand, "Miss Langston! So good to see you again, my dear!" Then the smile fled his countenance abruptly, "I'm so sorry about James. He was a good friend, and I miss him somethin' fierce."

"James was always very fond of you Mr. Webb. He had nothing but kind things to say about you," Dicey smiled into the man's gentle eyes that were accentuated by laugh lines extending out toward his temples.

Solomon entered the room, "Sarah would you and Liz be so kind as to serve some pie to our guests? Dicey, may I speak with you for a moment, dear? I need your help with something in my study."

Dicey passed the men, avoiding eye contact with Mr. Frederick as she did so. He always leered at her in a way that made her feel uncomfortable, and this occasion proved to be no different. Dicey left through the kitchen door to meet her father in the parlor, "Yes, Papa?"

"Please come with me for a minute, dear," Solomon limped back to his study with the aid of his cane, and Dicey followed him.

He shut the door behind them, limped to his desk and sat on the edge of it. The scent of leather bound books, pipe tobacco and peppermint permeated the room. Dicey stood facing her father, wondering why he had called her aside so suddenly, especially when he had guests in the home. His brow wrinkled and his eyes exuded anxiety and concern.

He spoke in soft tones, "Dicey, those men came here to pay their respects and they happened to mention in passing that they're heading over to Liz's father's house next to steal his horses. Mr. Frederick's horse got shot out from under him in a recent skirmish, and he's decided he wants Williamson's stallion for himself. They plan to take his other horses back to their friends. I tried to offer Frederick one of our horses, but he insisted that he's had his eye on Mr. Williamson's stallion for quite a while and he has his heart set on having him."

Dicey shifted her weight, obviously annoyed. In her mind theft was theft and it didn't matter if someone were an enemy or a neighbor. It had become common in those days to walk into a neighbor's home and find your belongings in use or your paintings hanging on their walls. Tories and Whigs alike raided each other's homes, making themselves welcome to whatever they felt a liking for. The whole practice infuriated Dicey and hearing that Mr. Webb would be involved in such a robbery disappointed her greatly.

"Richard may be a Tory, but he's a peaceable fellow and I don't want to see him lose his horses. I'd like for you to ride over, take Liz home and warn him. I'll stall them here for a while until you can get there and let him know."

"Certainly, Papa. I'd be happy to. I'll get Liz and leave now," Dicey took a few steps toward the door.

"Take your rifle and be careful, dear," he cautioned.

"I will Papa," she said and then opened the door and walked toward the kitchen.

"Liz, can you please come here for a moment?" Dicey called to Liz as her father followed her limping into the kitchen.

Liz walked past Solomon out into the parlor. Dicey took Liz by the arm and pulled her to the front door, "Come with me."

Puzzled, Liz accompanied her friend outside, "What is it, Dicey?"

"Come around to the stables with me," Dicey kept moving toward the back of the house to the stables.

When she got there she began to explain, "Papa wants me to take you home."

"Why? What's happening?"

"Those men in there intend to steal your father's stallion and Papa wants me to warn him," Dicey explained.

"My goodness!" Liz exclaimed.

"We need to leave quickly," she continued as she put the bridle and saddle on Gabriel. "Here, let me help you up," Dicey helped Liz onto Gabriel's back and then she climbed in front of her. "Hang on, 'cause I'm going to go as fast as we can."

Liz put her arms around Dicey's waist and the two girls rode off as fast as Gabriel could travel in the direction of the Williamson Plantation.

As they reached the Williamson property, Dicey tied Gabriel to the trunk of a large maple just inside the forest – the same forest where she'd overheard the Bloody Scouts discussing their planned attack on Little Eden months before.

"Why are you tying him here?" Liz questioned.

"I don't want to take a chance on the Whigs seeing him and recognizing him as my horse," she explained.

"Oh"

The two girls dismounted and ran to the front door and entered. "Follow me, Dicey. Father's usually in his study this time of the afternoon."

Dicey followed Liz through the corridor, past the large spiral staircase and toward Richard Williamson's plush study. The door to his study stood open, and the tall, distinguished gray-haired gentleman sat at his large ornate oak desk. He wrote intently with a quill on a piece of parchment.

Liz tapped lightly on the inside of his open door with her knuckles, "Father."

"Liz, dear, come in! I see you have a friend with you. Come in Miss Langston," he greeted with friendliness and sincerity.

"Father, we have some urgent news for you," Liz began.

His eyes rose in puzzlement, "You have?"

"Yes, Sir. My father sent me to warn you that a group of Whigs are on their way to steal your stallion and your other horses. They aren't far behind us. So you must act now to guard your property," Dicey explained.

"Indeed? How many are there?" he asked.

"Three, Sir."

Well, I must thank you, Miss Langston. And please send my gratitude to your father as well!"

"You're welcome, Sir. I will," she turned and left his study, Liz following her into the hallway. Mr. Williamson rose from his desk, walked to the door behind them and then called out into the hallway, "Bradley, will you come here for a moment please?"

Liz and Dicey watched as Mr. Williamson's servant, Bradley, entered his study and Mr. Williamson pushed the door. The door didn't quite close completely so as Dicey and Liz stood in the hallway, they could overhear Mr. Williamson's instructions to his servant, "Bradley, Whigs are on their way to seize my stallion and my other horses. Take measures to set guards on the horses. Have the men hide in the barn with their weapons and when the Whigs arrive, they can dispose of them. I'm tired of these rebels thinking they can attack anyone they please and steal their property."

Dicey's eyes widened as she stared at Liz. They both
understood the implications for the Whigs should they be
stopped by surprise.

"I must go," Dicey turned abruptly toward the front door
and Liz gently touched her shoulder.

"What are you going to do, Dicey?" Liz's concerned
voice fell to a whisper.

"I've got to warn them not to come here. I can't let them
get shot," Dicey whispered.

Dicey scurried toward the front door.

"Be careful, Dicey!" Liz whispered.

Dicey waved farewell as she ran out the door and toward
Gabriel. She untied him from the tree, climbed into the saddle
and took off toward her house along the path the Whigs
would most likely travel. As she rode, she realized that telling
them that Williamson knew of their plans would implicate
her. They would know that she had been the one to warn
him. She didn't relish the idea of facing William Frederick's
fury, but she liked Mr. Webb and didn't want harm to come to
him or the other man.

So she forged on in the direction she suspected they
would travel, praying all the while that she would have the
words and the courage to face Frederick. When she met them
along the way, the three men were riding atop two horses.
Frederick rode an old mare and Mr. Webb and the third man
shared another sturdy horse. As they approached, she
dismounted her horse and hailed them, "Hello, please halt,
Sirs."

"Miss Langston! We enjoyed your pie!" Mr. Webb smiled
and waved.

"Thank you, Sir," she accepted the compliment then continued, "I have something important to tell you."

"Yes?" Mr. Webb inquired.

"I just took my friend home to the Williamson Plantation and Mr. Williamson is aware of your plans to steal his horses. I overheard him say that he's setting men in wait to attack you when you approach. I would highly advise that you relinquish your plans and find an alternate source for horses."

The men glanced at each other and then Frederick spoke. "And how did they come to be aware of our plans, Miss Langston?" he asked irritably.

"I learned of your plans and warned him," she replied unabashedly.

Dicey could see the man's blood pressure rising as a large purple vein in his neck bulged and his face turned an even deeper shade of crimson than his hair. She solidified her stance and drew in a deep steady breath, bracing herself to withstand his wrath.

Frederick dismounted his horse, approached and glared down at her, his eyes blazing with fury. Seeing his associate's temper rising, Mr. Webb dismounted his horse and quickly stepped toward Frederick's side.

"I'm sorry, but Liz is my best friend and Mr. Williamson has been kind to our family. He may be a Tory, but he's a peaceable fellow in general and I couldn't stand by and let his property be stolen. So I warned him." Dicey stood bravely before Frederick – realizing that the man's temper could turn violent at any moment.

Frederick grabbed Dicey's chin in his clammy right hand, "Where are your loyalties, Miss Langston? I thought you were a Patriot!"

She defended, "I only wanted to stop the robbery, not cause you harm. When I heard that he planned to set a trap for you, I hurried along this path that I assumed you would travel so I could warn you."

"Thank you for informing us, Miss Langston. I suppose we could be angry with you now, but we can't fault you for being a loyal friend." Mr. Webb touched Frederick's arm in an attempt to calm him, "Frederick, we'll just have to find some horses elsewhere."

William Frederick jerked his arm away from him, "Shut your mouth, old man! I wanted that stallion for myself and now this silly girl has gone and ruined our plans." Frederick's venomous gaze darted over to Mr. Webb.

"It wasn't *our* plans. Smithson and I didn't want to steal the horses. It was your idea. It was *your* plans," Mr. Webb reminded, "Now leave the girl alone."

Frederick still clutched Dicey's face fiercely in his hand and leaned down until he peered maliciously into her eyes. Dicey held her breath, for his reeked of alcohol, "If you weren't James and Solomon Langston's sister, I'd teach you a thing or two about keeping your mouth shut!"

Mr. Webb, tugged at Frederick's arm, "Leave her be, Frederick, there's other horses. You can't fault her for protecting her best friend's father." Something flickered in Frederick's eyes that shifted from infuriation to a desire more sinister and salacious. The report of the poor Tory's wife who had been violated by the villain leapt into Dicey's consciousness. Terror gripped her more completely at that moment than it had at any other time, for she would rather take a bullet in the heart or drown in a river than suffer the degradation of an assault upon her virtue.

With renewed determination Mr. Webb interposed himself between the venomous deviant and the young woman. As Webb shoved Frederick's chest, the fiend released Dicey's face and she scurried back toward Gabriel and climbed into the saddle as the two men wrestling each other to the ground. Dicey did not linger to ascertain who would triumph. She ribbed Gabriel with her heels and he bolted homeward as fast as his legs could carry them.

When Dicey reached home, she ran straight into the house, bolted up the stairs and flung herself on her bed with her bedroom door shut behind her. She felt as if a hot searing firebrand were caught in her throat – the pain of holding back emotions for far too long. Satisfied that no one had observed her entering the house, she released the pent up anger, frustration and terror of all the raids, perils, and gunpoint attacks. None of them had distressed her as much as this singular frightful encounter with one who should have been a friend and ally, but rather was an insidious lascivious vermin. The entanglement of emotions at that moment brought forth a delayed reaction to every peril she had faced thus far and she sobbed bitterly, longing for Thomas' sturdy supportive shoulder and his arms to lovingly enfold her. Instead she was forced to settle for her feather pillow in which she buried her head and her uncontrollable sobs.

Thomas lay awake on his cot listening to the crickets chirp. He had removed his shirt and shoes and lay on top of his bedroll in an effort to stay cool. The hot, humid late-August nights made it difficult to sleep, but this night sleep would remain even more elusive than usual.

Thomas closed his eyes and pictured Dicey's face in his mind. Each night, Thomas would lie on his cot and think about what it felt like to touch her soft cheek, to kiss her sweet lips, to smell the perfume of her hair, or to feel her nestle her head into his chest as she embraced him. It had been two months since he'd seen her last, but he still found himself smiling as he thought about her dimpled grin and the way she blushed when she became embarrassed.

While thoughts of Dicey normally calmed him and helped him rest, tonight they only served to agitate Thomas. He restlessly rolled over onto his right side in an effort to get comfortable.

"Captain Springfield, I need you to lead an expedition into North Carolina tomorrow. Cornwallis has moved northward and set up camp in Yorktown, Virginia, but there are suspicions that he's left troops behind and we need you to take a unit of men and seek out their locations," Colonel Roebuck had instructed him a few hours earlier.

"This is an important mission, so I want you to select your best men," the Colonel directed.

Normally Thomas would have found this type of expedition a welcome challenge. He enjoyed the opportunity to leave the fort and head out on some dangerous adventure,

but tonight thoughts of Dicey made him hesitant. He kept
thinking of his last moments with her when she begged him
to be careful. Being careful and being courageous made
incompatible bedfellows in Thomas' mind. When he didn't
care what happened to him, he found it easier to be fearless;
but now that he had someone worth living for who leaned on
him and loved him, the stakes had changed.

Thomas rolled over to his left side and fought to cast away
the thoughts of Dicey which so habitually entered his mind.
*It's just an expedition. It's no great danger. I've gone into much
more hazardous situations than this before. I'll be fine. Dicey and I
will be together again soon,* he told himself over and over until
the exhaustion of the day's activities finally caught up with
him and he fell into a fitful slumber.

Thomas slept for several hours until shortly before dawn
when his dreams turned to Dicey. She slept at the base of her
favorite apple tree. He could see her so clearly, her brown
chestnut hair pulled back in French braids and her rosy
cheeks rising as a dimpled radiant expression spread across
her face. She wore a green dress with a white apron and
appeared as if she'd been cooking for flour dusted her hands
and apron.

Suddenly her image darkened as if several figures
hovered over her, casting their shadows down on where she
lay. Unexpectedly, a blood red apple fell from the tree over
her head and landed on her lap. A bullet hole had penetrated
the center of the apple and it oozed bright red blood onto her
white apron. She awoke from her slumber, caught sight of it,
looked up in horror at the shadowy figures standing over her

and cast the bloody apple from her chest. Her terrified
screams, "Papa! Papa! No!" pierced through Thomas' heart.

Thomas jerked upright in his bed, his heart pounding
furiously and his blood coursing through his veins. He
panted rapidly as his heart raced. "Dicey!" he called out. He
rubbed his hands through his wavy blonde hair which
dripped with sweat. He leaned his head into his hands as he
breathed deeply in an effort to calm himself. Gradually his
pulse slowed and the panic subsided. He continued to sit
upright in his bed, then put his feet on the floor and turned
up the low flame of his lantern to burn brighter.

What in the world was that about? he asked himself. The
bizarre dream left him strangely unsettled. Did it mean
something? Is Dicey in danger? Is her father or some other
family member in danger? Knowing that sleep would not
come easily now, Thomas dropped to his knees beside his cot
and began to pray for Dicey's safety.

~*~

Thomas and his small party of men traveled for several
weeks into North Carolina in a northeasterly direction
toward Yorktown, taking time to search the area thoroughly.
The information on where the enemy troops were supposed
to be appeared to be inaccurate, or old at the very least. One
muggy night in mid September they camped just outside of
Charlotte near the last known location of a regiment of British
regulars. The ominous gray clouds billowed across the sky as
if someone were unrolling a monstrous bolt of carpet across

the heavens. In the distance lightening flashed and the low rumbling of thunder echoed.

"It's comin' up a bad cloud. Let's pitch our tents here men," Thomas instructed. The soldiers were already soaked from traveling for miles in the soft rain. As the thunder grew louder and the lightning bolts grew closer, the men hurried from their horses and started setting up camp.

Thomas pulled a wedge of beef jerky from his pocket and took a bite, chewing it as he finished setting up his tent and ventured into a thicket of trees to gather firewood. He found an overhanging rock that had some dry pine needles sheltering under it, and gathered them for a fire. The other men gathered kindling and logs and with great effort they started a fire from the damp wood.

The men had just enough time to fry a batch of corn meal pancakes before the rains descended in a torrential downpour. They scrambled to their tents and Thomas retired to his by himself. He rolled out his bedroll, kicked off his boots, removed his rain-soaked shirt and pants and laid down. He rested with his hands behind his head and his legs crossed at the ankles as he listened to the thunder crack and the rain dance on top of his tent. The smell of the musty tent, the freshly falling rain, and the smoke from the rain-drenched fire filled Thomas' senses.

Thoroughly exhausted from the day's travels, the soothing sounds of the thunderstorm soon put him to sleep. He met Dicey in his dreams as he so often did. This time he accompanied her in the kitchen of her parents' home. They made donuts and both their clothes were dusted with flour. He teased her, eating the donut centers and stealing kisses from her as she fried the donuts. Suddenly a loud noise crashed in the front of the house and Dicey ran toward the noise. Thomas followed her, but his steps seemed slowed and exaggerated. No matter how hard he ran, he couldn't reach her. The distance seemed to grow farther and farther the more he ran. Finally, he found her in her father's study lying on the ground, shot in the heart and blood pouring from the wound. He lifted her into his arms, cradling her head in his lap. "Dicey, No, Dicey!" he cried aloud as he sat up, tears rolling down his face and his heart pounding severely within his bare chest.

He leapt to his feet, totally distraught, running his hands through his hair, "I've got to go to her!" he whispered aloud. "I can't keep traveling away from her. She needs me!" Thomas threw on his pants and boots and stepped outside of his tent. He began pacing around in the mud. The rain had stopped, the clouds had rolled away and the full moon shone down on him. *We're wasting our time looking for these troops. They aren't here and the farther I keep going the worse these nightmares get.*

When day broke, Thomas gathered his troops around the fire, "Men, I think we're wasting our time on this expedition. The information we were given appears to be either inaccurate or outdated. I'd like to hear your thoughts on turning back."

Three of the men immediately agreed with him and felt that they were wasting their time. They were tired and wet and they just wanted to get back to somewhere that provided shelter. But Thomas's trusted friend, Lieutenant Hammonds

169

disagreed, "Captain Springfield, I don't believe we can turn back now. We should thoroughly investigate the area indicated between here and Yorktown."

Two other men whom Thomas considered his trusted advisors agreed with Lieutenant Hammonds. Thomas stood by the fire and stepped a few paces from the men. His hand rubbed his beard-bristled chin pensively. He called back over his shoulder to them, "Let me consider the matter for a spell. Go ahead and put away the tents and load up the horses." He ventured further away from the men to a thicket of trees.

Please Lord, I don't know what to do he began to pray in his mind.

At that moment he felt a hand on his shoulder. Lieutenant Hammonds stood next to him, "What's wrong, Tom? I know you. This is more than whether or not we're wasting our time."

"It's nothing, Hank, really," Thomas lied.

"Don't try to fool me, Tom. Somethin's eatin' at ya and it's not just that we haven't found the British troops. Why do you want to turn back?"

"You'll think I'm crazy if I tell you," he shook his head in frustration.

"You're a levelheaded fellow. You may be a bit of a prankster, but you're not crazy," Hank smiled.

Thomas offered a fleeting smirk but immediately the anxiety returned to his expression, "It's Dicey. I keep having these recurring nightmares that she's in danger. And last night – last night it was absolutely horrible and no matter how hard I ran to help her, I couldn't reach her until it was too late. The farther I get from her, the worse the nightmares become. It's getting where I'm afraid to go to sleep."

A disquieting expression pervaded Lieutenant Hammond's eyes, "It's been nearly three months since you've seen her. Do you think it's just that you miss her?"

"I thought of that, but I think it's more than that. She's definitely in danger. It may already be too late." A tear glistened in the corner of his eye and he turned from Hank, wiping his eyes quickly and stepping further into the woods.

"So you think we should abandon our mission because you feel that Miss Langston's in danger?" Hank asked almost in a whisper.

"Yes, No – when you put it that way it sounds totally absurd, doesn't it?" Thomas slapped a tree trunk with the palm of his hand. "All right, we'll keep going. We'll check the area between here and Yorktown and then we'll head back. But we're moving fast, I tell you. No more dawdling."

"She'll be all right, Tom. She's a strong, smart girl and she has her family around her to protect her," Hank rubbed Thomas' shoulder with his hand. "You've made the right decision. Your duty has to come first."

"Then why do I feel like I just traded her life for my duty?" Thomas didn't wait to hear Hammond's reply, but stomped back to camp. The men looked at him quizzically as he returned.

"We keep going toward Yorktown."

~*~

171

Mid-morning on the 26th of September, 1781, Jacob Olsen tugged on Thomas's sleeve, "Captain, follow me. I've found the British."

Thomas followed the private as he led him to a cliff overlooking a lush green valley. Jacob descended to his hands and knees and crawled out on the ledge of an overhanging rock face. The private hung his head over the cliff.

"There, below," he whispered.

Thomas eased out onto the precipice and knelt down next to him. Sure enough, about 400 feet below camped a regiment of British soldiers.

"Well done, Jacob," Thomas whispered, "Get a count of how many men there are along with the number of horses, cannons and weaponry." Thomas quietly eased away from the precipice and when he'd reached more solid ground, rose to his feet and headed back toward camp.

"Hank, Jacob has found an encampment of British regulars just below the cliffs. My guess is that there are a few hundred of them, but he's getting a more accurate count."

"What do we do now, Captain?" Hank asked.

"We need to deliver a message to LaFayette at Yorktown. It's maybe a four-hour ride at full speed. I need for you to deliver it."

"I'd be delighted to deliver the message, Captain," Hank agreed.

"My guess is that they are holding some of their troops back here to come in as reinforcements and attack LaFayette's troops by surprise. Since they far outnumber us, I'll move the men away from here, about 2 miles west. We'll wait for you to return there and follow LaFayette's orders at that point."

"I'll prepare to leave."

"Get the full report from Jacob and then take Lieutenant Millan with you."

Jacob soon returned with his report. He'd counted 473 British soldiers with 6 cannons in the valley below them. Hammonds and Millan took off to meet LaFayette and Thomas directed his men westward as planned. They set up camp and avoided lighting a fire to insure that they were not spotted by the British.

About eight o'clock in the evening Lieutenant Hammonds and Millan rode into camp. Thomas, who had been pensively passing the time just outside his tent by whittling a willow to a fine point with his knife rose to his feet to greet them. "Did you find LaFayette? What did he say?"

"We found them. Washington and Rochambeau have just arrived to meet him with their troops. They're planning a full blown siege of Yorktown for the twenty-eighth. We gave them the location of the British troops and he seemed grateful to get it," Hank answered.

"What do they want us to do next?"

"He asked how many there were of us and I told him only seven. He said for us to return back the way we came and keep an eye out for more British troops coming up from the South. If we find any, we're to send a rider back to notify them at Yorktown. If we don't, we're free to return back to Woods Fort."

Thomas felt relieved that now there appeared to be a light at the end of the tunnel. He hoped and prayed there would be

no more troops – no more delays to keep him from returning
to Dicey.

~*~

It had been four months since Dicey had seen Thomas.
The last thing she'd heard from him was a letter delivered to
her shortly after he left Woods Fort to go into North Carolina.
When one month passed after another with no word from
him, she grew more concerned with each passing day. She
and Beth had corresponded regularly. If anyone understood
her anxiety about Thomas, Beth did. Dicey longed for the
heart-to-heart talks she used to have with her sister-in-law,
but she knew that it was better for Beth in Spartanburg where
the memories weren't so thick.

As fall descended, the trees began to change colors. Dicey
loved the fall of the year when the vibrant reds, oranges and
yellows burst from the trees in one last exultant sigh before
they fell from their limbs and the world became barren and
cold. The weather had turned chilly and Sarah kept Dicey
busy spinning, weaving and sewing clothes for winter. The
little ones quickly outgrew their clothes and not only did they
need new ones, but also Sarah and Dicey made shirts and
pants for the men who served in the military.

One cool October morning Sarah announced that she felt
they had enough shirts and pants made to deliver the
clothing to the troops, "Dicey, would you and Henry like to
take the wagon and deliver this clothing to Woods Fort?"

"I'd be happy to, Mama," Dicey looked at Henry. His
eyebrows rose, fell and rose teasingly. He knew that Dicey

hoped that Thomas had returned or at least that she could obtain word on his state of well-being from the men at the fort.

"Stop by Mrs. Williams' house on the way. She has some more to include with ours," Sarah added.

"Yes, Ma'am," Henry rejoiced in the opportunity to get out in the countryside and especially on a trip to the fort. He longed for the day that he would be old enough to join the military, but Sarah and Solomon hoped the war would end before any more of their children would be called to arms. Even if they weren't going to the fort, Henry would have been elated. Anytime he could travel with Dicey proved an enjoyable experience for him. Dicey made everything an adventure.

It took several trips for Sarah, Henry and Dicey to load all the clothing and blankets that they had prepared onto the back of the wagon. When they climbed aboard, Dicey let Henry drive the team while she sat back and listened to the clopping of horse hooves. Her dark chocolate eyes imbibed the vibrant colors and she inhaled the fragrance of autumn leaves as they rode through the countryside toward Mrs. Williams' home.

Henry drove the team up the long wooded drive toward Mrs. William' house and then stopped the wagon outside. Dicey hopped down from the wagon, sprinted up the front porch steps and rapped on the door.

Mrs. Williams cracked the door slightly, peered out and then flung it wide when she realized who stood outside, "Miss Langston! I'm so glad you stopped by! Your mother told me you'd be coming for the clothing and blankets for the troops. I have them right in here."

Mrs. Williams motioned Dicey and Henry into the house toward a sewing room in which were stacked large mounds of provisions. Dicey and Henry hefted piles of blankets and clothing and carried them to the wagon. It took several trips to complete the task.

"We have quite a load, don't we Henry?" Dicey's heart swelled as she observed the large supply of blankets and clothing they had gathered for the men. Among the items she carried with her, she held a blue shirt she'd made specifically for Thomas. She couldn't wait to see him wear it and knew that the blue in the shirt would accentuate his deep blue eyes. She kept that shirt separate from the others, lying beside her on the front seat of the wagon tied up in brown paper. She'd written "For Captain Thomas Springfield," on the outside and inside she'd enclosed a note to him. She hoped that she would have the opportunity to give it to him personally, but realized most likely she would have to leave it for him.

Henry drove the full distance to the fort and when they arrived, two guards greeted them and excitedly opened the heavy wooden gate to allow them to deliver their provisions. She asked the men at the gate whether Captain Springfield had returned, but they indicated that he had not.

Henry drove the team into the middle of the fort and Dicey hopped down and briskly approached the Colonel's cabin in hopes that he would have some word on Thomas. She knocked on the door.

"Who is it?" came a deep voice from inside.

"Miss Langston delivering clothing for your men, Sir," she replied.

Colonel Roebuck answered the door. The distinguished gentleman stood five-foot-eight, had a slightly protruding belly, and what hair remained around the sides of his head had turned a salt and pepper gray. His jovial smile twinkled in his hazel eyes as he welcomed her, "Come in, Miss Langston, Come in!"

Dicey stepped into the one-room cabin.

"So what do you have for us, Miss Langston?" the Colonel inquired jovially.

"We brought blankets, shirts and trousers for your men, Sir," she replied with a smile.

"How very kind of you! Those supplies are sorely needed," his grateful expression made Dicey feel warm inside.

"Sir, may I ask you a question?" she ventured.

"Why yes, Miss Langston, anything for you," he offered.

"Have you heard from Captain Springfield? Has there been any word?" she held her breath in hopes that the Colonel held some good news for her.

"I received a message from the Captain several weeks ago. He and his men made it all the way to Yorktown and received orders from LaFayette to search out more British troops in the area and return home. I haven't heard from him since, but I expect to see him walking in here any day now." The Colonel knew Dicey had lost James and understood her affection for Captain Springfield, even if she didn't realize he knew of it. "I'm sure he's fine, Miss Langston," he winked.

Dicey smiled, "Thank you, Colonel. You're very kind." She turned to leave the cabin and as she did loud happy shouts filled the air. Dicey and the Colonel exited the cabin and looked around to see what caused the commotion. A young man came running up to the Colonel, "Cornwallis has surrendered his entire force at Yorktown!"

"It's over!" shouted another man, "The war is finally over!"

The Colonel grabbed the man by the shoulders, "Hold on, son, what is all this?"

The young man who looked no more than fourteen breathlessly replied, "Cornwallis, he surrendered all of his troops to Washington and LaFayette at Yorktown. He gave up! It's over! The war is over!"

"Where did you hear this?" the Colonel asked, still unable to fathom that the War that had started over five long years ago could actually be over.

"Captain Springfield and his men have returned from their excursion to Yorktown and they brought the news!"

With the mention of Thomas' name, Dicey's heart leapt for joy, "Captain Springfield is here?" she interrupted.

"Yes ma'am, here he comes," the young man pointed toward the entrance of the fort where a tall, blonde man with a scruffy beard and ragged, dirty clothes strode toward them. Thomas raised his hand to block the sun from his eyes and strained to make sure that his vision had not deceived him. He began running toward them and went straight to Dicey, throwing his arms around her and lifting her into the air, kissing her cheeks.

"Uh hum" the Colonel cleared his throat, "Captain Springfield? Is that you behind all that dirt and hair?"

Thomas put Dicey down, but held onto her hand pulling it behind his back. He saluted the Colonel, "I'm sorry Sir. Yes, Captain Springfield reporting in, Sir."

"So what is this news, Captain Springfield? I'd like a full report," the Colonel turned to enter the cabin and motioned for Thomas to follow him. "You can give me that report now and then you can take some time to clean yourself up and visit with your friend."

Thomas turned to Dicey, "I'll be right back. Wait for me here," he whispered.

Dicey ran back to where Henry waited with the provisions.

"Was that Captain Springfield I saw passing me, Dicey? I hardly recognized him! He is so gaunt and he looks a lot different with a beard," Henry stared toward the cabin that Thomas and the Colonel had entered.

Dicey smiled enthusiastically, "Yes, Thomas is back! He's speaking with the Colonel and then I can see him. Did you hear the news?"

"I heard! Is the war really over?" Henry asked excitedly.

"I don't know, but it appears to be. If Cornwallis surrendered, then it sure sounds like it!" Dicey couldn't have had better news than that the war waned to a close and that Thomas had returned to her. She could hardly contain her jubilation. "Henry, would you mind terribly if we stayed for a while? I'd like to visit with Thomas as much as I can."

"Of course, I'm sure I can find something to keep me entertained around here," Henry thrilled at the opportunity to spend a day at the fort. He'd already found someone who'd offered to show him around.

Dicey left Henry to his exploration as she briskly returned to the Colonel's cabin and waited impatiently for Thomas to exit. She leaned against the cabin, her stomach fluttering with excitement as she nervously twiddled the drawstring on the bodice of her dress between her fingers.

Finally, after about thirty minutes, Thomas emerged from the Colonel's cabin and turned toward Dicey. He grabbed her hand and led her toward the fort's entrance, "Come on, I've got to get cleaned up." As he passed Dicey's wagon, he pulled a pair of trousers off the back of the wagon, holding them up to him. Satisfied that the pair he held would fit his long legs, he started rummaging for a shirt.

"Oh, don't worry about a shirt, I've got something just for you. She grabbed the package wrapped in brown paper off the front seat of the wagon and handed it to him. He stuffed the trousers and package under his arm and held her hand with the other as he excitedly left the fort and guided her into a nearby forest.

"Where are we going, Thomas?"

"The Enoree runs right along here. I'm going for a swim to wash a week's worth of dust off me," he continued to lead her along until they came to an embankment with the Enoree River running below.

"Isn't this a perfect spot?" The river rose about four feet deep and the shade of the colorful maple and oak trees that ran along the banks of the river provided a secluded escape for the couple. Large rocks on the side of the grassy embankment offered a peaceful spot to sit and dangle one's feet into the icy water.

Thomas let go of Dicey's hand, placed his trousers and package on a nearby rock, stripped off his boots and shirt and jumped into the water, "Woo, that feels good!" he exclaimed.

Dicey stood on the grass watching him splash around in the greenish-blue water. As he washed his face and long hair that now hung to his shoulders, the water glistening on his face and torso. How wonderful it felt to be with him again!

"Feel like a swim, Dicey?" he waved his arm for her to join him.

"It's too cool to swim today, Thomas. Aren't you freezing?"

"Nope. It feels wonderful! I don't care how cold it is. After weeks of traveling dusty roads, there's nothing like a good swim. You sure you won't join me?"

"Not today, Thomas, thank you," it did her heart good to see him not only alive and well, but also happy.

"Well, if you're not coming in…" Thomas reached down into the water, removed his trousers and flung them onto the grassy embankment.

"Thomas!" her face turned beet red and she covered her face with her small hands.

"I've been dreaming of that blush of yours for months. I couldn't resist seeing it again," he teased.

She spun around to look away from him.

"I'm under the water, Dicey. You're not going to see anything, and even if you did, I do have my under-things on. Turn around and let me see your pretty face."

Dicey gradually turned around and sat down on the rock facing him.

"So do you think the war is really over, Thomas?" she asked.

"Well, for the most part, yes. Cornwallis did surrender. I'm sure there will be Tories among us who won't give up that easily. We've had so much fighting going on amongst ourselves that people have developed some nasty habits. I'm not sure how long it will take for folks to learn to be civil with one another.

"I hadn't thought about that..." Dicey twiddled the draw string on her bodice nervously.

Thomas waded over until he stood waist deep in the water directly in front of her. "Now don't get all sad on me. For all practical purposes it is over. We may just need to watch our backs a little while longer." He reached up and put his hand gently to her cheek, "Oh how I missed you!" he exclaimed suddenly.

He took her face in his hands and kissed her, his scruffy beard scratching her face.

Dicey put her arms around his neck, "I missed you too, Thomas. When I didn't hear from you for so long I got so worried, and then mother asked me to bring the provisions and here you are – sent to me straight from heaven!"

"I worried about you too," he decided he wouldn't tell her about his nightmares. Why worry her when evidently they didn't mean anything? Here she sat in front of him safe and as beautiful as ever.

"You need a good shave," she rubbed her hand on his bearded chin.

"Yes I suppose I do, it's been awhile since I've had one. Now I'm getting a bit chilly here. Could you hand me my trousers, please?"

Dicey lifted them from her lap and handed them to him.

"Turn around for a minute please," he winked.

"Gladly," Dicey turned around and faced away from Thomas as he climbed out of the river, shook off the excess water and stepped into the trousers, pulling the draw string tightly around his waist and tying it in a bow.

"All right, it's safe now," he teased.

Dicey turned around to see him standing before her in his trousers, bare feet and chest and holding out his hand, "I assume that package has a shirt in it?" he smiled.

She nodded and handed it to him and he untied the string and opened the paper to find the note and the shirt inside. He held the shirt up to himself.

"I like it!" He wiped the excess water from his arms and chest with his hands and then slipped his arms into the sleeves. He didn't bother to button the shirt, leaving it hanging open in the front as he started reading.

Dicey watched him as his eyes went back and forth reading the note she'd written him. She hadn't planned on being able to be there with him when he read it. It made her a little self-conscious that he read it in front of her. She saw a smile spread across his face as he continued and then he folded the note neatly and placed it in his pocket.

He knelt down in front of her, facing her as he leaned his hands on the rock on either side of her.

"I love you too, Dicey," he whispered.

She wrapped her arms around his neck and toyed with the locks of wet hair on the back of his neck as she drank in the comfort and peace that she always imbibed from his deep blue eyes.

He leaned forward and kissed her gently on the lips and then he gave her the kiss that he'd been dreaming of every night as he lay in his tent. She put her hands on either side of his face and felt his strong jaw as he released the passion that had been pent up inside him for four long months.

After several minutes, she pulled back from him, slipped her arms under his open shirt around his bare chest and embraced him as she breathlessly chuckled, "Thomas you have to let me breathe."

He pulled her close to him, "I'm sorry. I just missed you so much. I didn't know if I'd ever see you again, and then today, there you were standing with the Colonel. It was an answer to my prayers."

She tilted her head back, worry filling her eyes as she studied his, "Why Thomas? Why did you think you would never see me again? Were you in danger?"

"Not for a minute," he shook his head smiling. "It was the most uneventful two months of my life. Other than finding one group of British regulars and sending a messenger to LaFayette to notify him of the location, it was utterly boring."

"Then why were you afraid you'd never see me again?" she asked a bit puzzled.

Thomas put his hands on her cheeks and searched her chocolate brown eyes, "Dicey, were you in danger at all while I was gone? Did anyone try to harm you or your family in any way?"

She shook her head, "No, no one. We've all been completely safe," her expression grew more puzzled, "What is it Thomas?"

He hesitated, "I just had a feeling that you might not be safe. It's probably just that I missed you so much, 'cause here you are safe and sound. I'm sure it was nothing." He shook his head and pulled her to himself once more, holding her tenderly in his arms.

Reluctantly releasing her, he rose to his feet, thrust on his boots, and began buttoning his shirt, "So did you make this shirt just for me?"

"Yes I did, and that blue looks as good on you as I thought it would," she smiled up at him.

"Thank you! I love it, Dicey," he took her by the hands and pulled her to a standing position, wrapped his arm around her shoulder and they walked back to the fort.

Chapter 9

"So you think I need a shave?" Thomas asked as he sat at his desk holding the looking glass up to study his reflection. He couldn't believe how gaunt his face had become over the last two months.

Dicey stood behind him and fiddled with his blonde locks, "Definitely, and something's got to be done about this hair. It's entirely too long."

Thomas pulled open his desk drawer, retrieved a pair of scissors, a comb, a straight edge and shaving soap, set them on the desk and shut the drawer back. He held the scissors and comb up to hand them to her, "Well then do something about it. You know how to cut hair?"

"I've occasionally cut my brothers' hair," she took the scissors and comb from his hand.

Dicey combed through his hair which hung in wavy locks to his shoulder, pulled it up between her fingers and snipped. As she continued to comb and cut his hair, he closed his eyes and relaxed so much that he nearly fell asleep.

At one point, he sat so still and quiet, that she put her hands on his cheeks, turned his head slightly, and peered around to look at his face, "Are you awake, Thomas?"

"Uh hum.. that just feels so nice and relaxing I thought I'd take a little nap," he mumbled.

Dicey walked around to face him and studied his beard, "Hmmmm… what to do with this?" She began trimming the beard back with the scissors and then walked over to a table, picked up a water basin and brought it back to the desk.

"Do you want me to do this? Or do you trust me with a straight edge?" she asked with a mischievous smile as she jiggled the razor in front of him.

"Completely, go right head" he enjoyed her doting on him. He'd risk a nick or two for the pleasure of having her near him.

Dicey's hands trembled slightly as she fidgeted with the straight edge. She had helped shave her father when he returned home wounded from the war, but that had been several years earlier, so she felt a bit jittery.

Thomas grabbed her wrist and winked at her, "Now stop that shakin'. You're making me nervous."

"It's been a while. Are you sure you don't want to shave yourself?" she held the straight edge out for him to take it.

"I trust you. I usually nick myself anyway. You can't do any worse."

She lathered the soap in her hands and spread it generously onto his cheeks, chin and upper lip. Then picked up the straight edge and told herself, *Calm down. You've done this before, you can do it again.*

Her hand steadied and she shaved him without making a single cut.

"Well now you can never leave me," he grinned as he studied his reflection in the mirror and wiped the shaving soap from his face with a towel.

"Why's that?"

"I'm spoiled now – a clean shave without a single nick! You'll have to stay and shave me every morning," he chuckled.

He set the mirror down and pulled her to himself, "I just can't stop drinking in your beauty, Dicey. Imagine you being here the day I return! Heaven must be smiling on me for sure!"

She took his face in her hands. He looked even thinner now without the beard, "You need fattening up, my love."

"I need you to bring me some of those famous donuts of yours," he smiled.

"I will. I'll come back and bring you a batch as soon as I can. I'm not waiting months before we see each other again. Mother will just have to resign herself to the fact that she can't keep me cooped up sewing and spinning day after day."

Dicey looked out the window where the sun lowered in the sky. "Speaking of Mama, she's probably worried about us. Henry and I were just supposed to drop off the provisions and return home directly," she explained.

"It will be sunset soon. I guess you really should be going. I don't want you traveling at night," he rose from his chair and held her hand as they walked to the door and outside to the front of the fort. Henry lay in the back of the wagon taking a nap.

"Poor Henry, he's fallen asleep waiting for me," she patted her brother's head.

Dicey leaned her back against the wagon and turned to face Thomas.

"Thank you for cutting my hair, and I love the shirt," he bent down and kissed her gently.

"You're welcome, Thomas,"

He enfolded her in his arms and held her tightly for a full minute before he whispered softly into her ear, "Be careful, Dicey."

The haunting tone of his voice startled her, and she pulled her head back to search his eyes that were glistening with emotion, "What is it, Thomas?"

"Nothing, just please – please be careful," he kissed her on the cheek, released her from his firm embrace and helped her into the wagon. Dicey turned the wagon around and drove out the entrance to the fort. He stood watching her as she rode away. She turned and blew him a kiss and he waved at her just before the soldiers closed the gates behind her.

~*~

Dicey changed into her nightgown, untied her braids and brushed out her long wavy chestnut tresses as she sat on her bed. She stood and placed her brush on her dresser and walked over to the chair where her dress and apron that she'd worn earlier in the day lay. She lifted her apron to pull out a lock of blonde hair and went to her dresser where she pulled a ribbon from her drawer. Tying it around the lock of Thomas' hair, she then placed it in a small tin inside her dresser drawer for safekeeping.

She went back to her bed, fluffed her pillow, blew out the lantern and lay down for the night.

~*~

Thomas plopped down on his cot, pulled off his boots, his toes wiggling, celebrating their freedom from the confining leather boots. He reduced the flame of his lantern to a low flicker and relaxed on his back with his hands behind his head and his legs crossed at the ankles. Finally he would have a good night's rest. The war was over, Dicey was safe, he was back close to her, and all would be well now. No more waking up in the middle of the night in a cold sweat from nightmares.

He closed his eyes and quickly drifted off to sleep. Hours passed in peaceful slumber. Dicey entered his dreams as she ambled through the orchard, gathering apples from the trees on a beautiful fall afternoon. She climbed up into an apple tree and collected the fruit in her apron. As she reached up to grasp a dark red apple, a snake slithered and dangled from a tree limb, its bloody fangs hissing right in front of her face. She panicked and slowly pulled away, descended the tree and plopped to the ground only to find four more serpents hissing at her at the base of the trunk. Each of them had blood dripping from their fangs.

She screamed, "Papa, Papa!" and ran toward the house, through the kitchen door, into her father's study and found him shot, lying in a pool of blood on the study floor. Dicey ran to her father, lifted his head onto her lap and then pulled her hand back to find it soaked with bright red blood, "Thomas, help me!" her voice sounded no louder than a broken tearful whisper, "Thomas, where are you?"

Thomas sat up in his bed, his heart pounding, his pulse racing and his breath laboriously rapid. He ran both hands through his neatly cropped hair, sprang to his feet, paced a few steps, and then leaned his clenched fists on his desk, breathing heavily. Grimacing, he pounded his fist onto the desktop, "Why? Why am I still having these nightmares?" he whispered aloud.

He could ignore the dreams no longer. A sense of urgency filled his entire body. He threw on his trousers, flung his arms into his blue shirt, and thrust one foot after the other into his boots, hopping on one foot at a time as he did so. He grabbed his hat and coat, and left the cabin, buttoning his shirt and jacket as he sprinted to the shelter where they kept the horses. He put the bridle on his horse's brown snout and secured the saddle in place. Hopping upon the animal quickly, he galloped to the front of the fort where he met two men standing guard.

Jacob asked, "Captain Springfield, where are you going now? It's only about half past three."

Thomas answered authoritatively, "I'm riding to deliver a warning. I'll be back in about three hours. If I'm not back in four, send a handful of men in arms to the Langston Plantation." Thomas knew that it took an hour to get to the

Langston's, an hour to return, and if he spent an hour with her, he could make it back in three. If it took much more than that, then his worst fears would have become a reality.

"Understood, Sir," Jacob replied as he opened the gate and allowed Thomas to ride through.

Thomas rode as fast as his horse could carry him by the light of the full moon, and he made the trip a little faster than planned. As he approached the Langston Plantation, he slowed his steed in an effort to keep from waking the entire household. He dismounted his horse and guided him around to the back of the house, putting him in the stable in an empty stall next to Gabriel. He thought it best not to alert anyone to his presence by having his horse standing tied up outside.

There stood a large maple tree that grew up behind the house and its limb forked over in front of Dicey's bedroom window. Thomas reached up and placed his hands on two lower limbs on either side of the trunk and pulled himself up until he had climbed into the tree. He carefully worked his way over to the limb that extended out in front of her window and peered inside to see her sleeping soundly in her bed. He hesitated for a second. He hated to wake her for she looked so peaceful, but then with renewed urgency he tapped on the window. Dicey didn't stir and so he rapped again a little harder. She sat up in her bed, peering toward the window with a puzzled expression. Recognition lit up her face and her mouth dropped.

"Thomas!" she gasped in a light whisper. She rose to her feet, threw on her shawl that lay on the chair next to her bed, pulling it around her as she hurried to the window and opened it. "Thomas, what on earth are you doing here in the dead of night?" she whispered. She couldn't decide whether to be worried or thrilled as her heart raced at the sight of him.

"May I come in? I need to talk with you."

She stepped back and allowed him to enter the room. By the moonlight streaming into her bedroom, she could see the anxiety on his face, "What is it Thomas?"

"It's kind of a long story. Can we sit down and talk for a few minutes?"

She walked to the table next to her bed and turned up the lantern from a low flicker to a moderate flame, and then pointed for him to sit down in the chair next to her bed. She sat down on her bed facing him and tucked her feet up under her.

"You're making me nervous, what's wrong?"

"Remember when you asked me why I was afraid that I would never see you again and I told you that I had a feeling you might be in danger?" he began.

"Yes."

"Well, there was more to it, but I didn't want to tell you because I assumed that since you were safe that it was all just me worrying for nothing."

She stared at him in silence.

"Dicey, I've been having dreams about you for two months."

"I've been having dreams about you for a lot longer than that," she chuckled in an effort to lighten the dark mood.

"These are nightmares, Dicey." Thomas' voice became so insistent that any mirth she felt from her last comment vanished. "I have three dreams that reoccur almost nightly. They alternate, and there's scarcely a night that I don't have one of these dreams. They started the night before I left to go north."

"Really? What are they?"

Thomas hesitated. He didn't know how much to tell her, "In one dream you're asleep in the orchard and a blood red apple is shot through the center, lands on you and blood oozes from it. You scream out for your father and run in the house. In another, you're in the kitchen cooking with me, we hear a loud noise, you run to the study, but I can't catch up with you. For some reason, I can't make my body move to help you. Finally I reach you and you've been shot, lying in a pool of blood in your father's study.

Dicey's heart pounded and she started to feel queasy, "Thomas!" she gasped.

"I know... and in the third, you're in the orchard again picking bright red apples – blood red apples - and then a snake with blood dripping from its fangs dangles down and startles you. You back down the tree only to find four more bloody fanged snakes hissing at the bottom. You run, screaming for your father into his study, where he's been shot, and then you call out for me to help you."

"How horrible, Thomas! And you've dreamed these every night for two months?" she gasped.

"Yes, at least one of these dreams every night. They are engraved into my mind. I've studied on them. I've tried to discern what they mean. I've looked for the commonalities," the frustration in his voice became evident as he continued, "In each dream, you are dusted with flour and appear to have been cooking. Two of the dreams have apples in them and there are three endings – in the first an apple is shot. In

194

the second you are shot, and in the third your father is shot. Your father seems to be a common factor in all three dreams. You either call out to him or run to him. In one dream I'm with you in the kitchen but I can't reach you and in another one you call out for me to help you."

"What do you think they mean?"

"I don't know for sure, but it's obvious that you and your father are in danger, and evidently I'm not going to be much help to you." Thomas hung his head disappointedly and then looked up to continue, "The danger may come while you're in the orchards or while you're cooking. Your father's study also seems to be a possible location for danger."

"What about the snakes?"

"I don't know – They're just in the one dream. There are five snakes with blood on their fangs and one is separated from the other four." Thomas paused and then exclaimed, "Oh!" He remembered something.

"What?"

"In the dream where you're asleep in the orchard, there are five shadows cast down on you as if there are five people standing over you. Maybe the snakes are people who intend you or your father harm?"

"Thomas, this is scaring me."

Thomas rushed over and sat next to her on the bed and put his arms around her, "I know, I'm so sorry to come here and alarm you like this in the middle of the night, but I felt this urgency that you needed to be told immediately."

"It's not your fault, Thomas. You can't help that you've been tormented by these awful nightmares. You did the right thing to come and warn me."

Thomas continued to hold her in his arms, "Now that I've told you about it ..."

She finished his sentence, "What do we do?"

"I don't know. Maybe just knowing that danger could be lurking will help you in some way. As much as I want to, I can't stay with you."

"How *did* you manage to get away?" she pulled back to look into his face.

"Fortunately, Jacob stood guard when I left. I told him I had to carry a warning and that I would be back in three hours. I even told him that if I didn't return in four to send armed men to your house."

"Really? Armed men to our house?"

"I can't explain it. I expected the dreams to stop when I returned and saw you, but then I went to sleep and woke up with the dream about the snakes. I just had this overpowering urgency that the danger is close and there's no time to be lost in warning you. I knew the Colonel would never approve of me leaving the fort just because of my dreams. So I saw the cover of night as my only chance."

Dicey hugged Thomas around his chest and leaned into his shoulder, "I'm so sorry, Thomas. I'm so sorry that you've been tormented so."

"It's not your fault, Dicey," he comforted.

"I know, I just hate that you've had to endure this," she clarified.

He put his hand under her chin and guided her face up to look into his eyes, "Dicey, if it would help you, I'd endure it every night for the rest of my life. I wish it were me in danger instead of you or your father. I love you more than anything in this world." He pulled her to himself again and held her tight. Being in his strong and capable arms soothed away the fear for the moment, and she inhaled deeply filling her senses with the essence of him.

"When do you have to leave?" she whispered hesitantly.

"I don't know. I don't know what time it is. Jacob said it was around half past three when I left, so I'll need to leave here by half past five."

Dicey stood up and crossed to her night table to retrieve her watch, "It's about fifteen 'til five. It's time I started preparing breakfast. I left some donuts rising overnight. If we hurry, maybe I can cook a few before you have to leave," she smiled.

"Oh, now that sounds good!" Thomas' face brightened.

"Would you mind stepping out into the hall while I quickly get dressed?"

Thomas rose and walked to the door, "I'll be right outside."

Dicey quickly pulled off her nightgown, put on her green dress and her apron and placed her watch in the pocket of her apron. She picked up the lantern and crossed to the door and opened it to find Thomas waiting outside. He followed her down the stairs and to the kitchen. Dicey set down the lantern and handed Thomas an apron. He tied it around himself as she carried the bowl of dough to the kitchen table.

"Thomas, can you please hand me that canister of flour over there," she pointed. He carried it to the table and she lightly dusted the surface, removed the cloth from the bowl and pulled out a large ball of dough and plopped it onto the flour-dusted table.

"Let's speed this up, will you please light the fire in the stove and get that pot of oil going for me while I roll out the donuts?"

"Yes ma'am," he cheerfully lit the stove and loaded a few pieces of wood to get the stove hot enough to boil the oil.

Then he returned to Dicey who had already cut out several donuts. She pulled the pocket of her apron open and said, "Pull my watch out of there and keep it so you can keep track of the time."

He reached in and took out the watch, "Right at five o'clock," he announced. "My mouth's watering for some of those donuts," he smiled.

She held a donut center between her thumb and forefinger and held it out toward him to eat it. He leaned forward and ate it from her fingers, "Mmmm, thank you!" he mumbled with his mouth full of dough and bent over and started to kiss her mouth.

"All right now, none of that, we've got work to do," she teased, "Go check on that oil and see if it's getting hot yet."

"Yes ma'am," he responded as if he were following orders from the Colonel.

He leaned over the oil studying it, "How do I know if it's hot enough?"

"Does it have little bubbles coming up through it?"

"A few," he answered.

She held out another small donut center, "Here, put this in there and see if it starts to cook."

Thomas reached over, grasped the dough and pretended that he planned to eat it.

"Uh uh – in the oil, Thomas," she teased scoldingly.

He smiled broadly and dropped it in.

"Looks to be cooking to me," he answered.

Dicey picked up three donuts and went over to the stove and dropped them in, "Looks like you'll get your donuts before you leave."

As Dicey worked frying the donuts and pulling them out to drain on brown paper, Thomas stood behind her with his arms around her waist, occasionally steeling kisses from her cheek and neck.

"Do you want donuts for breakfast or kisses, Thomas?" she finally asked.

"Both," he smiled.

She spun around to face him, "What time is it now?"

He pulled her grandfather's watch out of his pocket and flipped it open, "I've got ten more minutes."

She reached over, grabbed a donut and put it in his mouth, "Donuts now, kisses later," she winked and then turned back around to pull more donuts out of the oil.

She picked up a donut for herself and returned to sit at the table, "I'll take a break from frying. I can finish the rest of this after you're gone."

Thomas sat down at the table facing her, he felt as if he were experiencing déjà vu. This whole morning in the kitchen duplicated the one in his dreams. Even the green dress! She wore the flour-dusted green dress and white apron!

Thomas began to feel sick and set his donut down on the table in front of him.

"What is it?" she noted the anxious expression on his face.

"This is all too familiar," he shook his head.

"That's because we've made donuts together before, remember?"

"No, this is like my dream," he mumbled. He rose to his feet and began pacing the floor, "I can't leave — I can't leave you now."

She stood up and put her hands on his waist in an effort to settle him, "Thomas you have to go. You told Jacob to send reinforcements if you didn't return. You can't have them showing up here just to find us kissin' in the kitchen," she grinned in an effort to lighten the mood.

"Uggh" he grunted, "Why did I tell him to do that? I could have stayed if I hadn't done that!"

"Thomas, you wouldn't be having these dreams if something couldn't be done about them. Why would God warn you if it can't be changed? Perhaps you telling me has already set in motion a series of events that will alter everything," she tried to sound like she knew what she was talking about for his sake, but deep down she knew she was really trying to convince herself. She didn't want him to leave her, but she didn't want him getting in trouble with the military over her either.

Thomas pulled the watch from his pocket, "It's time to go," he thrust it back into his pocket and pulled her to him, "Can I have my kisses now and take my donuts with me?"

Dicey put her hands around his neck and pulled his face towards hers. She could feel the sadness in his kiss, "Thomas, I'll be fine. We'll be fine." She turned and wrapped up a half dozen donuts in brown paper and handed them to him, "You better go now."

He held the donuts in his left arm, pulled her to him with his right and kissed her as he never had before, gently, lovingly as if she were a delicate treasure that he dare not break, "I love you Dicey" he mumbled into her hair as he held her in a firm embrace, breathing in the sweet scent of her.

"I love you too, Thomas. Everything will be fine, you'll see," she offered comfortingly as she kissed his cheek.

He walked past her to the kitchen door, and out, turning around to wave goodbye. As he walked to the stables, she followed him as far as the kitchen door and then shut and latched it behind him.

Dicey plopped down in a kitchen chair, put her elbows on the table, and held her head in her hands as tears rolled down her cheeks.

Thomas entered the stable door and patted his horse on the neck, "Hey there, boy" he greeted gently. He heard the sound of breaking glass, a stinging blow to his head, and then everything went black.

~*~

Thomas lay unconscious in a mound of hay. His hands were tied behind his back, his feet tied together and his mouth gagged with a cloth tied around his head. Matthew Love and four other Bloody Scouts sat in a circle nearby.

"Grab those donuts, Matt." Ned Turner, a lanky auburn-haired man of perhaps twenty-four, pointed to the donuts wrapped in brown paper that Thomas had dropped when he fell. Matt retrieved the package, unwrapped the donuts, took one for himself and passed the remainder to Ned. Ned took one and handed them to his older brother Dick, who gave the rest to Curtis and Aaron Mills.

"It's a shame to have to kill a woman who can cook this good," Aaron said as he took an exaggerated second bite of his donut.

"Kill her?" Matthew's head perked up. "We aren't killin' women and children here today are we?"

"Cunningham said to do whatever it takes to rid the world of the Langston men. If we get rid of them, we can take this fine plantation here for ourselves. My thoughts are we need to eliminate the heirs. If that means women and children, so be it," answered Aaron. His brother Curtis nodded his head. Curtis and Aaron were twins. They both had sandy brown hair, were broad shouldered with double chins and beer bellies from hanging around in the taverns guzzling ale.

"I don't see that that's necessary," Matthew responded, "If we get rid of the old man and the older sons, then the women and children can just be kicked out of the house. They won't stand a chance against us."

"Ah, but it's cleaner to just dispose of them all," Dick chimed in as he wiped his pug nose on his sleeve.

"Cleaner? Is that what you call it?" Matthew grew irritated, but he tried not to show it.

"Maybe Matt's right," Ned offered, "Maybe there's no need to kill women and children, but one thing's for sure, this feller over here's gotta go." He pointed to Thomas who still lay unconscious.

"That's right. He's been sniffin' around Miss Dicey for months and the last thing we need is him marrying her and considering himself an heir to this plantation," Dick rose from his seat on a bail of hay and pulled his knife from a sheath that hung on his belt as if to finish the deed that very moment.

Matthew sprang to his feet and caught Dick's serpent-branded forearm, "Now hold on, Dick, I think this fella may prove useful to us yet if we keep him alive."

"How you figure that?" Dick halted looking quizzically at Matthew Love.

"I think we can use him to motivate young Miss Langston and the others to leave. If she's as infatuated with this fella as I think she is, she'll do whatever is necessary to spare his life," Matthew explained.

"Now that's using your head, Matt!" exclaimed Ned. "I like that idea."

"So what's our plan?" Dick awaited Matthew's response.

"Well, let's see here. The Langstons will be rising for breakfast soon. There's only so long a body can sleep with the smell of those donuts waftin' past your nose. We'll wait until after they have breakfast and then we'll wait for the old man to enter his study. Then we'll bust down the front door, take him by surprise, kill him and then deal with the others as needed."

"What about him?" Dick pointed to Thomas.

"After we've disposed of the old man and have the others in check, Dick, you can run back here, and bring him into the house with a gun to his head. We'll demand that they either vacate the premises immediately or we'll blow his head off," Matt explained.

"I like it. I think it'll work just fine," Ned concurred, and the others nodded their heads in agreement.

~*~

Dicey finished pulling the last donut from the hot oil as her father, mother, Henry, Bennett, Celin and Amy entered the kitchen.

"Yum, donuts!" Celin exclaimed.

"Nothin' like Dicey's donuts – eh, Papa?" Henry smiled.

"That's right!" Solomon agreed.

"Sarah, I have some work to do in my study, I think I'll take a plate of these in there and eat them as I work," Solomon placed three donuts on his plate and limped back to his study.

Henry had already wolfed down one donut and worked on his second, "I'm gonna go check on the new foal out in the stables, Mama."

"Fine dear," Sarah smiled at her son as he grabbed a third donut and stuffed it in his shirt pocket. He hurried out the door to the stables and opened the gate, making his way to the new foal born the day before. As he passed Thomas' horse, he took a double take and came back to him, patting him on the nose.

"What are you doing here, boy? Where's your master?" just as he turned around to look for Thomas, he felt a heavy blow to his head and darkness closed in around him until he lost consciousness.

"Now wasn't that handy," Dick gloated as he pulled the donut from Henry's shirt, stuffed it in his mouth and drug Henry over to lie next to Thomas.

"Tie him up, Aaron, would ya?" Dick directed.

Aaron took a rope from his pocket and bound Henry's legs and arms and stuffed a dirty handkerchief in his mouth.

"Ned - you head around toward the front of the house and see if the old man's in his study yet," directed Matthew. "Be careful that you're not seen through any windows and when he's there, come back and tell us."

As Dicey and her mother cleaned the kitchen, Dicey began hesitantly, "Mama, I have something I need to tell you."

"Yes dear?" she looked at Dicey's worried expression, "What is it?"

"Thomas came to me in the middle of the night."

Her mother's eyebrows rose, "He did?"

"Yes, he's been having horrible nightmares that either Papa or I are in danger. He's had one practically every night for the last two months and last night he had yet another one. He felt such a sense of urgency that I should know of the danger that he came and warned me. He left soon afterwards so he'd arrive at the fort before anyone noticed."

"What kind of danger, Dicey?"

"Life threatening," Dicey swallowed hard.

"What does he think we should do?" Sarah asked with concern.

"I don't know, but at the first hint of any trouble, please promise me, Mama, that you will take the little ones upstairs and hide them. Don't think or worry about anyone else. Just

205

get Bennett, Amy, Celin and Henry upstairs as fast as you can," she begged.

"But what about you and your father?" Sarah didn't know what to think.

"We'll take care of ourselves. But if we have to worry about the little ones getting hurt, we're liable to make a mistake and it – it could be fatal," Dicey warned.

"My heaven's Dicey! Do you really believe his dreams mean something?"

"I think they do, Mama. It's really got Thomas worried."

"I think you need to tell your father, dear," Sarah suggested, wringing her hands nervously on her apron.

"You're right, I'll go tell him right now." Dicey put down the dishtowel and walked toward her father's study. As she entered the doorway, she heard a loud crash and realized that the front door now lay flat in the entry way. The five Bloody Scouts poured into the house, headed for the study and Dicey ran to her father's side.

Sarah, upon hearing the crash, gathered her three children who sat finishing their donuts at the kitchen table. She lifted Amy and Bennett into her arms and instructed Celin to hang onto her skirt. As she saw the five men enter the house, she feared that she would not be able to get the little ones past them unnoticed.

She scanned the room. Remembering the cellar, she scurried to open the cellar door and helped the three children down the stairs. She shut the door behind them, and pulled them over to huddle in a corner behind shelves of provisions.

Meanwhile in the study, Dicey stood next to her father who had risen from his seat and now positioned himself resolutely behind his desk.

"What do you men want here?" he demanded authoritatively.

"We want your house and lands, old man," Aaron stated coldly.

"What in the world makes you think you have a right to our land and home?" he asked incredulously.

"Because when you're dead, and we've kicked your family out of here, this will all be ours for the taking," Aaron waved his arms around and then stepped forward until he stood barely a yard from Solomon. He pointed the pistol at Solomon's heart and cocked the weapon.

"No!" Dicey's shriek was so blood curdling that she didn't realize that it had come from her own vocal chords. She jumped in front of her father and shielded him with her own body.

"Get out of the way, Miss Langston, or the contents of this pistol will be lodged in your own heart," Aaron demanded.

Dicey, threw her arms loosely around her father's neck, "You'll have to shoot me first. I will not move."

Matthew Love looked from Dicey to Aaron and back at Dicey, "Aaron, remember, we decided not to kill women and children," he stated calmly.

"If it's the only way to rid the world of Solomon Langston and the foolish ideas that he's spoon-fed his children all these years, then so be it. We wouldn't have even had to endure this blamed war if it hadn't been for the likes of him," Aaron threatened.

207

"Aaron, put the weapon down. It's over," Matthew tried to calm his partner in crime.

"You're a fool, Love. I think you're as gone on this filly as the feller out in the stables," Aaron pointed the pistol at Dicey's heart and just as he started to squeeze the trigger, Matthew Love, pushed Aaron's arm out of the way and the pistol went off, dislodging its contents into a painting of a bowl of apples that hung on Solomon's wall.

Within seconds, armed military men poured through the door of the Langston home, seized the Bloody Scouts, relieved them of their weapons and tied their hands behind their backs.

Dicey ran to Matthew Love, "He mentioned Thomas, Mr. Love. Where is he? Has he been harmed?"

As an officer held Love's arms behind his back and tied his wrists together, he revealed, "He's out in the stables. He's tied up, but he's alive."

"Thank you, Mr. Love. Thank you for saving my life."

"We're even now, Miss Langston. I've paid my debt to you," he nodded as the military officers took the Bloody Scouts out the front door.

Dicey ran through the house and out the kitchen door to the stables. She saw Thomas' horse next to Gabriel, put her hand on the horse's neck and asked, "Where's Thomas, boy?" She scoured the stables with her eyes, working her way back to the corner where Thomas and Henry lay. Henry still lay unconscious, but Thomas struggled to free himself from the ropes that bound his feet and hands.

"Thomas!" Dicey rushed to him and reached behind his head to untie the scarf from his mouth and pulled back her blood-drenched hand.

"Thomas, your head is bleeding!" she gasped and wiped her hand on her apron.

"There's a knife in my pocket," he lifted his hip for her to reach inside his pocket. She retrieved the knife, opened it and cut the ropes from his wrists and feet. He grabbed her by the shoulders, "Are you all right? Is your father? I heard the shot!"

"We're fine, Thomas. The pistol went off and the bullet lodged in a painting of apples on Papa's study wall," she reached over and cut the ropes that surrounded Henry's wrists and arms and removed the cloth from his mouth.

"A painting of apples – well, well," Thomas marveled.

"Poor Henry! He's out cold!" she exclaimed as she hovered over her brother's unconscious body.

"I didn't see who got us. Who was it?" Thomas felt utterly bewildered.

"The Bloody Scouts - there were five of them. Here, help me carry Henry into the house," then she turned to look at him, "Or can you? You probably need to be carried yourself!"

"I'm fine. Got a hum dinger of a headache, but I'm fine," Thomas lifted Henry in his arms and carried him.

"This boy's heavy to be so wiry!" Thomas panted.

"Let me go get you some help," she offered, "You're probably weak from loss of blood."

"No, I've got him, just open the doors and let's do this quickly before I pass out," Thomas hurried toward the stable doors with Henry in his arms.

Dicey opened the door and ran ahead to open the kitchen door.

"Here, bring him in here in the parlor," she pointed.

Sarah Langston peeked her head out of the cellar door when she heard Dicey's voice.

"Oh my! Henry!" she exclaimed as she saw Thomas carrying him into the parlor. She hurried to her son and the three little children trickled out of the cellar door one by one behind her.

Solomon stood at the front door speaking with the military officers, and Thomas joined them as Dicey and Sarah tended to Henry.

"Thanks for coming, Jacob," Thomas shook Jacob's hand in gratitude.

"It's a good thing you told us to come here if you didn't make it back. We got here in the nick of time," Jacob shook his head looking at Thomas and then at Solomon, "So where were you, Captain Springfield, when your damsel was in distress?" Jacob teased.

Thomas rubbed his head, "Knocked out cold, I'm afraid. When I prepared to leave earlier this morning, they knocked me over the head and tied me up. I woke up about the time the shot went off."

"You've been in the stables all morning, Captain?" Solomon rubbed his beard, a bit puzzled.

"It's a long story, Sir. I'll tell you about it later," Thomas smiled.

"If it has to do with you being with my Dicey in the middle of the night, I better hear about it sooner rather than later," Solomon scolded.

Dicey joined Thomas and the officers at the front door and Solomon stepped aside to seek out his wife and Henry.

Dicey noted with concern, "Thomas, your head wound is still bleeding. We need to tend to it."

"Jacob, can you please let the Colonel know that I will be here until I can have my head wound attended to and then I will return to the fort?" Thomas asked.

Jacob tugged Thomas's shoulder turning him to look around at the back of his head. He whistled and exclaimed, "Captain, that looks pretty bad! I think you better stay here and rest a few days," Jacob affected grave concern and then winked at Thomas.

Thomas rubbed his head and agreed, "Hmmm, maybe you're right Jacob."

Dicey saw the blood on Thomas' hand, "Come with me in here in the kitchen and let's get you cleaned up." She grabbed his clean hand and led him to the kitchen where her mother had already set some water boiling.

"How is Henry?" Thomas asked.

"He just woke up. He's got quite a lump, but he isn't bleeding like you are. Mama's putting him upstairs in his room to rest."

"Take off your coat. It's covered with blood," she instructed, "Maybe if I clean it right away, we can keep it from staining your uniform."

Thomas handed her his coat and she set it on the back of a chair. Dicey mixed some boiling water into a basin of cool water and began cleaning his wound.

"My goodness, Thomas! What in the world did they hit you with? You've got such a large gash here."

"I think they hit me with a liquor bottle. I saw broken glass in the stable," he answered.

"I better check for glass then," she studied his wound carefully and cleaned it gently. "I don't see any glass, but I do believe that I should put a few stitches in here to close up the wound."

Dicey hated stitching wounds, but it had to be done. She ran upstairs to her mother's sewing area, gathered scissors, needle and thread and brought them downstairs to begin the task.

"I'm so sorry, Thomas. This is going to sting," she prepared him before she started.

"That's fine, just do it quickly," he asked as he braced himself, leaning his head on his folded arms which rested on the kitchen table.

She pressed the wound closed and sewed the flesh together the best she could with four quick stitches and bandaged his head to stop the bleeding.

"There, I'm done." Thomas lifted his head from his arms and scooted his chair back from the table. She walked around to stand in front of him. His long legs stretched out on either side of her as she gazed down into his eyes, "Thank you, Thomas."

"For what? I wasn't a lick of help," he shook his head, disgusted with himself.

"Yes you were! Because I was prepared, I warned Mama and she got the children to the cellar safely. If she'd run into the midst of everything, she or one of the children could have been harmed. Being prepared also helped me keep my wits about me."

"Dicey, I believe you *always* have your wits about you," Thomas wasn't convinced he'd made much of a difference by telling her his dreams.

"You never know what would have happened had you not warned me. What if you hadn't come? Then Jacob and the other men wouldn't have been here to help."

"I suppose you're right. Yes, that's true," Thomas began to feel more confident that perhaps his being knocked out in the barn proved of some worth in the end. "I'm just so relieved that you're all right," he held her hands in his and pulled her closer.

Solomon Langston entered the kitchen to find his daughter in a passionate embrace with the Captain, "My word, Captain, when are you going to just ask her?"

Dicey jumped back at the sound of her father's voice, "Ask me what?" She stared at her father, then at Thomas and back to her father.

"You two carry on around here like a couple of love sick hounds. When are you just going to ask her to marry you and be done with it?" Solomon's hearty deep voice boomed.

Dicey's face flushed and Thomas glanced over and chuckled to see her blushing. He felt a bit red-faced himself. She was surprised to hear her father suggest such a thing – especially after the conversation she'd had with him about Thomas' father.

"Well, Sir, would you give me permission if I were to ask you for it?" Thomas inquired.

"Hmmm…" Solomon pretended to be weighing a great dilemma, "Let's see, you do tend to disappear at the moment of crisis, but overall, you're a good-hearted, hard working fellow. I think my answer would have to be in the affirmative." A smile spread across Solomon's face.

Dicey's mouth dropped open, flabbergasted that her father stood right in front of her coaxing the man she loved to ask her to marry him. Did he not think it would ever happen without his meddling? She felt so annoyed, yet simultaneously relieved that he had accepted Thomas in spite of his past.

"Now don't be letting Papa talk you into something you're not ready for, Thomas," Dicey felt the need to give Thomas an escape route.

"He's not talking me into anything I hadn't already thought about," Thomas turned to Solomon, "Thank you for your permission, Sir. Dicey and I will talk this over and get back with you on our decision." Thomas decided to remain in control of the situation. He sensed that it was important to Dicey that it be his choice to ask her and not her father's coaxing.

Solomon rolled his eyes, "Young folks!" he shook his head, turned and left the kitchen.

"One moment," Dicey held up her finger to Thomas and quickly followed after her father and tugged him toward his study. Once inside, she shut the door behind them.

"Yes?" Solomon queried with a hint of confusion.

"I thought you didn't approve of Captain Springfield and now you're twisting his arm to marry me?" Dicey's eyebrows furrowed.

Solomon shrugged his shoulders, "I never said I didn't approve of Captain Springfield. I just suggested you weigh the possibility that he might share his father's unstable tendencies."

"Does this mean that you are no longer concerned about him?"

"I spoke with your mother and she told me about his coming here to warn us. I believe Captain Springfield has satisfactorily proven himself to be courageous, dutiful and quite stable," Solomon nodded.

"Then you approve of him?"

"Yes, you have my blessing where Captain Springfield is concerned... that is if he ever gets up the nerve to ask you for your hand!" Solomon rolled his eyes.

Dicey rushed to her father, flung her arms about his neck and kissed his cheek. "Thank you, Papa! Thank you!"

~*~

Dicey and Thomas sat together on the bench below the weeping willow tree by the pond. The sun beamed down, providing warmth on an otherwise chilly afternoon. Thomas stayed to recover from his head wound, but not one word had been said by either of them about marriage since her father's prodding two days earlier.

Dicey started to worry that Thomas didn't want to marry her, but that didn't make sense. Yet, why had he been so silent on the matter? She decided it wasn't her place to bring up the subject, so she resigned herself to waiting until Thomas broached the subject himself.

Thomas turned sideways on the bench to face Dicey, "I've been doing a lot of thinking and with all the hostilities going

215

on right now, I think it's important that I stay in the military until things are under control."

Dicey could feel the disappointment rising within her.

He continued, "The Colonel told me it could take a year or more before any kind of treaty is signed. If I stay in the military for another year, I can save up my wages and be able to buy a good piece of property when I get out. What do you think?"

Dicey hesitated. What was he trying to say to her? "I think you're right about the hostilities continuing for a while and that you are needed in the military. I also think that it would be wonderful if you could save your wages and buy a piece of property when you're out."

"Would you like to have a plantation like your Papa's one day?" he asked.

"It's a lot of hard work, but I love all the fruit trees," she looked across the pond to the apple-laden orchard.

"I figure we can take the money that I have saved up from the military, buy a small farm, build it up, sell it for a profit and purchase some land to build a fine plantation like this," he planned.

"We", he used the word "we!" she thought to herself. Dicey wished Thomas would do as her father directed and just ask her.

Thomas reached into his pocket and pulled out her grandfather's pocket watch, "I believe this is yours."

Dicey took it from his hand, "Oh yes. Thank you." She held the watch, rubbing the smooth gold in her hands.

"Got any secret messages in there?" he winked.

"No," she replied.

"Are you sure about that?"

She looked at him a bit confused until she saw his mischievous smile.

"Maybe you better double check," he suggested.

Dicey opened the watch and exposed the secret compartment. Taken by surprise, she found a small folded piece of paper inside. She nervously pulled the paper from the compartment, closed the watch back and placed it inside her apron.

"Wonder what that is?" he affected surprise.

Dicey slowly unfolded the piece of paper and read it, "*I love you Dicey Langston. Will you be my bride?*"

Dicey clutched the paper in her hand, flung her arms around his neck and kissed him.

"So is that a yes?" he smiled.

"Yes! Yes! Yes!" she kissed his cheek repeatedly and hugged his neck.

"So you'll wait for me to get out of the military? You won't run off and marry someone who's more handsome and who doesn't disappear in a crisis?" he teased.

"Yes, I'll wait for you!"

"Thank you, Dicey! You've made me the happiest man in the world." Then, he leaned over and kissed the brave girl who would one day bear his children. Together they would bring forth a freedom loving posterity who would honor and revere her for centuries to come.

Epilogue

Thomas Springfield and Laodicea Langston were married on the 9th of January 1783, in Laurens District, South Carolina. King George issued his "Cessation of Hostilities" the following month and the treaty ending the Revolutionary War was signed September 3, 1783.

Ten years after their marriage, Dicey and Thomas bought land on the west side of the Reedy River in Greenville, South Carolina near Traveler's Rest, and built their plantation and their lives together

Dicey lived a long and happy life with the man she loved and together they had twenty-two children. Later in her life, Dicey gladly boasted that at that time she had thirty-two sons and grandsons capable of bearing arms, and ready at any time to do so in the maintenance of that liberty which was so dear to the youthful heart of their ancestor.

Dicey died on May 23, 1837. Her obituary read:

"Died on Tuesday, the 23rd, Mrs. Laodicea Springfield, aged 71 years, wife of Thomas Springfield. The deceased was the daughter of Solomon Langston of Revolutionary memory, whose family perhaps suffered more from the ruthless ravages of the Tories and Indians than almost any other, and the subject of this remark took an active part in the struggle and performed many daring deeds on behalf of her suffering country and friends. She was the mother of 22 children and has left about 140 grand and great grand children. She was a kind and affectionate wife, mother, and neighbor, and has left a large circle of acquaintances to deplore her loss."

The author feels humbly honored to be the fourth great granddaughter of Thomas and Dicey Springfield through their son Solomon Langston Springfield

Monument

Today there stands a monument in Traveler's Rest, South Carolina erected in honor of Dicey Langston's bravery. The epitaph on the stone reads:

On this site
Stood the Home of
Laodicea Langston Springfield ("Dicey")
1759-1837
Heroine of The American Revolution
To her daring and courage
Many Patriots owed their lives
This Rock was a hearthstone in her Home
Erected by The Nathaneal Greene Chapter D.A.R.1933

A newer bronze tablet with a correction for her birth year was added some years later and its dedication reads:

Laodicea (Dicey) Langston
May 14, 1766 – May 23, 1837
Wife of Thomas Springfield
July 15, 1766 – March 21, 1845
Corrected, 1966

Directions to Dicey Langston's D.A.R. Marker:
Highway 25, just north of Traveler's Rest, South Carolina, turn right onto Old Tigerville Road. Approximately 1.5 miles, the Marker is in the front yard of a private residence on the right side, just across the road from a Baptist Church.

Learn More about Dicey at http://www.DiceyLangston.com

Bibliography

Clement, J. editor, 1859 Noble Deeds of American Women, with Biographical Sketches of Some of the Most Prominent., C.M. Saxto, 25 Park Row, New York, NY, in 1859

Norfleet, Phil, *Biographical Sketch of William "Bloody Bill" Cunningham,* extract from an article entitled *"Random Recollections of Revolutionary Characters and Incidents"* by Judge J. B. O'Neal; this article first appeared in the *Southern Literary Journal and Magazine of Arts,* Vol. 4, No. 1, July 1838, pages 40-45

Elliott, Elizabeth, Women of the Revolution (Vol. l Pages 284-291.) (available in Kennedy Library, Sptg., S.C.) Second edition published in 1848 by Baker and Scribner, 36 Park Row and 145 Nassau Street, New York, Volume I, Chapter XXII – Dicey Langston.

Ellis, Joyce Howard and Pollard, Ann, *Springfield Family 1739 -2001,* 2 vols., Baltimore: Gateway Press, Inc.

Family Bible of Thomas and Laodicea Springfield

About the Author

Marnie L. Pehrson was born and raised in the Chattanooga, Tennessee area. An avid enthusiast of family history, Marnie integrates elements of the places, people and events of her family's heritage into her historical fiction romances. Marnie's life is steeped in Southern history from the little town of Daisy that she grew up in to the 24 acres bordering the famous Chickamauga Battlefield upon which her family resides. The Chickamauga Battlefield inspired her book *Rebecca's Reveries* and e-book *Back in Emily's Arms* available through CleanRomanceClub.com

The Patriot Wore Petticoats, was her first foray into historical fiction. From the moment she learned that Dicey and she were born exactly 200 years apart to the month, Marnie, a mother of six, has felt a bond with the heroic mother of 22 children! It was Dicey's remarkable life story and encouragement from friends and family that persuaded Marnie to branch out of her inspirational writing to venture into historical fiction romance. With her inspirational writing background, you can always count on a moral to every story.

Marnie and her husband Greg live with their six children in Ringgold, Georgia. She is the founder of multi-denominational SheLovesGod.com which hosts the annual SheLovesGod Virtual Women's Conference the 3rd week of October each year. She is also an internet developer and consultant who helps talented professionals deliver their message to the online world. You may visit her projects through www.PWGroup.com or reach her by email at webmaster@SheLovesGod.com or by phone 706-866-2295.

MARNIE L. PEHRSON

Other Books by Marnie Pehrson

Rebecca's Reveries
Historical Fiction
224 pages, paperback, ISBN: 0-9729750-2-0
Rebecca Marchant had led a sheltered life until she found
herself inexplicably drawn to the home of her father's youth.
Surrounded by the historical landscape of the Chickamauga
Battlefield in Georgia, Rebecca finds herself plagued by
haunting dreams and vivid visions of Civil War events. As
Rebecca walks a mile in another girl's moccasins through her
visions and dreams she learns about compassion, forgive-
ness, temptation and the power of true love.

Lord, Are You Sure?
ISBN 0-9729750-0-4, 152 pages
A roadmap for understanding how Heavenly Father works in
your life, helping you understand why certain problems keep
repeating themselves, how to break the cycle and unlock the
mystery of why you encounter challenges and roadblocks on
roads you felt inspired to travel.

10 Steps to Fulfilling Your Divine Destiny: A Christian Woman's Guide to Learning & Living God's Plan for Her
ISBN 0-9676162-1-2, 124 pages
Have you ever said to yourself, "I'd love to do great things
with my life, but I'm just too busy, too untalented, too ordinary, too afraid, too anything but extraordinary"? Inside this
book you'll learn how to reach your full God-given potential.

If you enjoyed *The Patriot Wore Petticoats*, you'll love
http://www.CleanRomanceClub.com

Journal/Workbook Companion for
10 Steps to Fulfilling Your Divine Destiny:
A Christian Woman's Guide to
Learning & Living God's Plan for Her
ISBN 0-9676162-2-0, 220 pages

Packets of Sunlight for Parents
Compiled by: Marnie L. Pehrson
144 pages, paperback
ISBN 0-9676162-4-7
Brighten your day with inspiration for parents of tots to teens!

Packets of Sunlight for American Patriots
Compiled by: Marnie L. Pehrson
ISBN 0-9676162-3-9, 108 pages
Let the founding fathers, reignite your love for
freedom!

A Closer Walk with Him
SheLovesGod Study Lessons Volume 1
by Marnie L. Pehrson
212 pages, paperback, ISBN 0-9729750-3-9
A collection of insights and ponderings on the scrip-
tures and how we can apply them to our everyday
lives. Great for the faith-lift you need in the morning,
just before bed, or whenever you need a quick boost of
inspiration. Each lesson is self-contained and
independent. Read them in any order the Spirit moves
you or read the 52 lessons in order as a yearly study
guide - it's up to you.

To order call 800-524-2307 or visit
www.SheLovesGod.com/bookstore

Printed in the United States
52937LVS00002B/103

9 780972 975049